Ed Ashurst (signature)

Kidnapped

Mystery and Collusion in the Bootheel of New Mexico

A Novel By

Ed Ashurst

A gift from Jim and Colleen

Kidnapped

Mystery and Collusion in the Bootheel of New Mexico

A Novel By
Ed Ashurst

Published by Granite Peak Productions, LLC

Other Books By Ed Ashurst

Non Fiction
Miracle or Coincidence?

Real Cowboys: Grand Canyon to Mexico

Wagon Boss:
A True Cowboy Story

Mavericks

The Life and Times of Warner Glenn:
A Glimpse into the American West

Alligators in the Moat:
Politics and the Mexican Border

Charlie Gould: Memories of a Cowboy

Stories that Terrell Shelley Told Me

Mel Potter and Friends

Fiction
Stealin' From The Neighbors

Order of Chapters

"Evidence becomes irrelevant."

Thomas Sowell
From his book *The Vision of the Anointed*

Chapter One
January 7, 2016

O n a rocky hillside on the southern edge of Hidalgo County, New Mexico, a lone man sat nestled in a rock pile holding a pair of binoculars, frequently putting them to his face and pointing them off to the south looking for something. It was cold, and scattered about intermittently were patches of frozen snow, perhaps an inch thick and sometimes more but never exceeding four inches. Where there was no snow, scant vegetation rose up out of the rocks and gravel, a bunch of dry tabosa grass here and there; and frequently rising higher out of the ground there were scrubby juniper trees, and off in the distance, several miles and lower in elevation, the predominant shrubs were mesquite, catclaw, and greasewood. In between his purposeful periods of surveillance the man added a stick or two to his small fire that lay hidden amongst the rocks. He made sure to use old dead wood that would create little or no smoke, and he kept the fire inconspicuous and small in size. He was hiding. He was also quite sure of himself as a well-trained soldier would be. The fact that he was hiding did not mean that he thought he would be caught by whomever or whatever he might be hiding from. He had no intention of being apprehended. He was not an amateur.

From his hideout he could see the Sierra Madre, the mother of all mountains, rising up in elevation from the low spot several miles below him known as the San Luis Pass. This place, this country, was a pitiful place compared to the Sierra Madre that he gazed at way off in the distance. In the Sierra one did not care about borders. Were you from Chihuahua? Were you from Sonora? Up there, a hundred miles south of where he lay hidden with his binoculars, Chihuahua or Sonora wasn't as important as your kinship to the Sierra. He was from there. It was his home and he wished he could stay there. This place, the United States of America, was only a place to make money, and unlike many of his Mexican comrades, he had no desire to be here other than to make money. Los Estados Unidos was a place to make money, dinero, but la Sierra, that was a place to live.

The man whose name was Vidal Garcia Pizarro was a Mexican and one member of a larger group, perhaps a dozen or more, who had breached the international boundary between the United States and Mexico and traveled north in a convoy consisting of five pickup trucks, each loaded with a total of twelve to fifteen hundred pounds of high-quality marijuana grown in the Mexican state of Chihuahua and headed toward markets to the north. Markets in Phoenix, Denver and Chicago. The marijuana in this particular convoy had a street value in cities like Chicago or Denver totaling somewhere between six and ten million dollars, so the soldier nestled on the hilltop holding the binoculars was not involved in a smalltime operation. This was big business.

Vidal wore a uniform colored in the shades of camouflage and had a very military appearance. Laying in the rocks several feet away from his crouched position was a Romanian manufactured AK-47 semi-automatic

2

rifle complete with a 30-round magazine. In his backpack amongst his other plunder, such as canned sardines and orange-flavored Jumex juice, was a second and fully loaded 30-round magazine. Also in his possession was a cell phone and high-quality satellite radio. He had the ability to talk to his comrades a mile or two away as well as to his superiors located south of his position where they sat in a ranch house on the northern frontier of the state of Chihuahua about twenty miles away. It would not be untrue to say the man was well connected.

Vidal Garcia Pizarro had been raised on, and still possessed, a small ranchito west of the Chihuahuan town of San Jose Babicora. His ranchito sat in the Sierra on the very line that separated Chihuahua from Sonora in a steep and rugged place, a wild place where one could go downstream on the west side of his ranchito and end up in the Gulf of California or if you went downstream from the east side of his ranchito you would find yourself on the shores of the Gulf of Mexico. He had a wife there, a beautiful wife and two children, a boy and a girl. He had a few cows and a few horses and a garden. Sometimes he found work in a nearby gold mine, sometimes as a hunting guide for rich Americans who came to shoot whitetail deer or turkeys. But as often as he could afford to, he just stayed at home and worked for himself. He was always happy there.

When he was a boy it had been peaceful in the mountains, but then things slowly changed. Because of the United States' insatiable appetite for drugs, local farmers began growing opium poppies and marijuana, and then a lot of the farms and ranches were bought by the cartels; and the cartels and the culture that they promoted changed the landscape. The cartels brought guns and fear. Honest people who wanted nothing to do with the Narco business either shut up or moved away, and the Narcos slowly took over until they ruled with an iron fist. A man did not have to be involved in the drug business, but he had to ignore it and keep his mouth shut. The agrarian economy changed from corn to narcotics, and with the narcotics came the introduction of the AK-47 rifle. People who grew corn had no AK-47 rifles, people who grew opium poppies and marijuana did.

Vidal did not grow opium or marijuana, but he had joined the Narco army. He was always a very good outdoorsman, a natural leader, fearless, and gifted with more intellectual possibilities than most of his peers; so over a period of years and several trips up the trail as a mule with dope on his back, he became a guide and then a scout, one who looks for the enemy, which in most cases was the United States Border Patrol. In his career he had made about thirty trips north of the Mexican line, sometimes going up the spine of the Peloncillo Mountains on the Arizona/New Mexico border and sometimes going up the spine of the Continental Divide and the Animas Mountains. He had been as far north as Interstate 10 between Lordsburg and San Simon ten times. He had been over the top of the Chiracahua Mountains in Cochise County three times and had been where he could see the lights of Willcox, Arizona at night. He had never been caught by the Border Patrol and had never been robbed by anyone from a rival cartel. He had never shot or killed anyone, but he knew he could. He had become something of a legend among the kingpins of the Juarez Cartel because of his stellar record as a scout and guide, that and the fact that he was smarter than most. But Vidal was not a ruthless killer or a sadist. He held no animosity toward Americans, and he preferred the crisp clean air and wild slopes of the Sierra Madre and his little ranchito to being inside the boundaries of the United States of America. He was involved in the drug trade for one reason only, and that was to make money. Being a scout and guide for the cartel was not a career many would aspire to, but he was the best in the business and the cartel bosses recognized that, and they paid him well. Far more than others who did the same job.

Vidal was, along with his comrades, a soldier of the Juarez Cartel who had most recently, and conveniently, purchased a large cattle ranch that lay against the international boundary on the Chihuahua side. This ranch, besides being a good investment to use up some of the millions of profit in American dollars that the cartel was enjoying, provided a perfect staging point for product that was, although illegally, being exported into the United States. These soldiers of fortune had congregated at the cattle ranch owned by the cartel and loaded the five 3/4 ton pickups with three and a half tons of marijuana that was neatly packed into cubicle bundles which varied in size from five to fifty pounds. These bundles were tightly wrapped in burlap and plastic.

The men left the ranch and drove on Mexico's Highway 2 that ran parallel and south of the international barrier from Agua Prieta, Sonora to Janos, Chihuahua, which was about fifty miles southeast of their position. They traveled to a spot on Highway 2 where a two-track dirt road went north a distance of two miles and came to a wire gate on the barb wire fence which at that particular spot was the only physical barrier separating Chihuahua, Mexico and Hidalgo County, New Mexico in the United States of America. This gate was about eight miles due west of the port of entry at Antelope Wells. The route traversing this same gate had been used extensively by illegal aliens, some on foot and some in vehicles, who wished to enter the United States unannounced or unencumbered by inspection from anyone at the Antelope Wells Port of Entry that was itself some forty miles south of Hachita, New Mexico and New Mexico's Highway 9 and sixty miles south of Interstate 10.

When the five-truck caravan had passed through the wire gate it proceeded in a northwesterly course up the White Water drainage and across the western edge of what was known as the McKinney Flat. After several miles they reached a well-maintained dirt road known locally as the San Luis Pass Road, and then after continuing west for a mile or so, they turned due north on a road of lesser quality but still passable going toward a cow camp called the Lynch Ranch. Where the Lynch Road left the San Luis Pass Road was about six miles due west of another cow camp named the Culberson Ranch and approximately two miles east of San Luis Pass which crossed over the Continental Divide at a low spot twelve miles south of Animas Peak at 8531 feet in elevation.

Going south from San Luis Pass, the Continental Divide rose up and entered Mexico's mysterious Sierra Madre, the mother of a thousand legends of terror and splendor and the location of Vidal's ranchito. This spot was one of the wildest and most untamed places left anywhere in North America, certainly in the land south of the Canadian border. If one drew a circle with a radius of twenty miles, having San Luis Pass at the center, one would never find a consistent population exceeding thirty people. If one totaled up every soul from the Continental Divide east to the bottom of the Playas Valley and stretching from the Mexican border north to Highway 9, an area of 600 square miles, a total of fifteen permanent inhabitants could not be counted, and sometimes there was half that number.

Hidalgo County, New Mexico was an area covering 3,446 miles and had a population totaling 4,240 people, and 95 percent of them lived in the northern half of the county which meant 212 people lived in the southern half. These 212 people were scattered over 1,102,720 acres. Another interesting statistic was that in an area stretching from the Mexican border north, a distance of eight miles and from the Arizona border going east twenty-miles, an area of about 150,000 acres, the continuous population never exceeded eight souls; and a good deal of the time, they were not home. It was lonely out there. The hombre with the binoculars perch was eight miles north of the Mexican border and two miles east of the Continental Divide. To the north and 8 degrees west, a distance of nine miles, Animas Peak rose up 2,500 feet above his position.

The Narco caravan consisted of ten men, two in each of the five pickup trucks. The Juarez Cartel had been sending drugs north through this territory for decades, usually on the backs of men, fifty pounds at a time, and sometimes in trucks one or two at a time. But for several reasons they had decided to launch five trucks at once on this trip. One reason being they were confident they could rely on some help, especially in the first thirty miles, from some influential people. The second reason being that the product they were importing was worth so darn much money. Greed played a big part.

The men had been sent forth with a topographical map showing a new route up the east side of Animas Peak on roads they thought would be passable. Usually the routes they used for drug-laden vehicles went on more widely used roads including the Cloverdale Road that went up the west side of Animas Peak and then on to the bottom of Animas Valley, by several ranches, and finally reaching the village of Animas. More often they sent trucks east to New Mexico Highway 81 going on to Hachita. But this caravan, the largest one ever pointed north, was going up the primitive ranch roads that hung close to the boulder-strewn slopes of Animas Peak on its east side.

Many tons of dope had been packed north through this same area on the backs of men, but no one on the ten-man crew of this caravan had ever traveled on these primitive roads in a vehicle of any kind. A route traveled on foot doesn't necessarily look the same as when seen from the window of a pickup truck.

For the first hour or so, everything went perfectly. The outlaws did not encounter any agents from the United States Border Patrol, which was how it was supposed to be. They turned north off of the San Luis Pass Road headed toward the Lynch, but then before reaching that destination, they encountered a new road, which had been made by a bulldozer and other equipment, veering off to the left. This was somewhat confusing to the man who was acting as the pilot holding the topographical map while seated in the cab of the first truck. They stopped and palavered. This new road seemed to be more widely traveled, and therefore it must be an easier route, or so they thought.

After considerable deliberation they decided to take it, and in doing so they headed west; then after perhaps a mile, the new road turned to the north. This made the men happy because, although they didn't know exactly where it was going, they were relieved to be on a northerly course. They drove on, and after several miles they found themselves descending down a winding road into a canyon, and when they reached the bottom they saw a water well. There was a small windmill tower and a large steel-rimmed water storage with about 30,000 gallon of capacity. The well and storage sat in the bottom of the shallow canyon, and when the first truck in the caravan rounded a corner in the winding road leading down into the spot and the well came into view several hundred yards away, the pilot gave the order to stop. He looked at his map and then lifted his eyes and surveyed the countryside. This must be the place on the map called Birch Springs.

He had not expected to be here and realized that following this new road that wasn't shown on his map had created this unexpected turn of events. But according to the map, there was a road going on toward the north that would eventually bring them back onto their desired course. After some minutes of study and comments from his companion behind the steering wheel, he decided, perhaps, this was even better than what they had planned. It looked like by going this way they could avoid the Lynch Ranch. Were there people living at the Lynch? The intelligence that had been gathered had told them no, but then they couldn't be sure. After several minutes of thought, he decided that this was an unforeseen stroke of good luck, and he told his companion to proceed further, and the truck creeped forward down the rocky road toward the well and water storage.

They traveled slowly, not being sure where exactly the road left the well site, but then found a primitive looking two-track road going up the ridge on the other side of the creek and decided it must be the one shown on the map; but they could not see where it crossed the rocky creek bottom. They turned downstream staying on the near side for several hundred yards, and then they spied the depression in the steep bank at the creek's edge and could tell that was where the primitive road crept on. They drove up to the creek's edge, and looking forward they could tell there had been little or no traffic for a long time.

The road was not much more than exposed rock where tires from vehicles had killed the grass and other vegetation. That was of little concern because their tires were good and the trail seemed to be pointed the correct direction. The pilot gave orders to proceed, and as the truck descended down the creek bank the two men could see a small trickle of water flowing gently down the bottom, mixed with a considerable amount of mud. The water was obviously coming from the open-top water storage that had been overflowing for many days. There was little or no thought given by either man, in this the lead truck of five, considering the water or mud in the creek. It did not look dangerous. But then when the front tires of the overloaded truck encountered the mud and trickle of water they immediately sank six inches. The truck almost stalled, and instinctively the driver pressed hard on the accelerator pushing the front tires forward and sinking deeper with every inch. For a split second the truck seemed unshackled when the tires escaped the mud to the far side, and the driver pressed even harder with his right foot and that brief burst of energy sent the truck lurching forward, and the rear tires entered the flood plain.

With 1500 pounds of prime marijuana resting on top of the rear axle, the tires reached new depths unexperienced by their mates attached to the front axle. "Aye Cabron! Quitar el arroya hombre!" The tires spun, and the engine roared, and the rear axle sank down to the springs. The truck stopped. "Chingar su madre!" The pilot was now screaming, "Que esta's haciendo?" He slammed the topographical map against the dashboard. He cursed as he threw the door on the passenger side of the truck open.

The truck had sunk so low that the bottom of the door almost touched the mud and gravel. The pilot looked at the sunken rear tires and he cursed some more. Other men were scrambling out of the pickups that had been following and various comments ushered forth, all of which contained sufficient profanity. And then, on top of all their other problems, it started snowing.

The ten men were unprepared for this type of trouble. They had ventured forth with two men occupying each of the five trucks, but the extra man in each truck was there, for more than any other reason, to act as extra security. There was at least one semi-automatic weapon in each vehicle. Most of the weapons were semi-automatic pistols, 1911s or Glocks. Vidal Garcia Pizarro who was riding shotgun in the third was the only man with an assault rifle, the AK-47.

Guns were about the only tools the Narcos had in their possession. They did not have one shovel or any type of tow chain or rope. There were no wrenches with the exception of a lug wrench for changing tires, but they did have three sets of simple pliers and a good set of wire cutters. The one thing they had a lot of was very good electronics. Every man had a cell phone, and they had four high-quality satellite phones, and they immediately put them to use. Especially the jefe.

The jefe, Ray Martinez, the boss of the caravan, was as different from Vidal as a Thoroughbred horse would be to a Clydesdale or a skunk from a bobcat, except for the fact that he, Ray, was also well known, but for different reasons. He had grown up in the barrios of Cuidad Juarez and had gone the way of a criminal when a young boy. He had been a member of a gang by the time he was ten. In the barrio where he spent his early childhood, there were hundreds of thousands of poor people living in the most abject poverty where opportunities for social and economic advancement were nonexistent.

Ray Martinez never knew who his father was. His mother had five other kids to raise and probably none of them would ever learn who their father was. By the time Ray turned twelve, he had left home and was dealing drugs, stealing what little he could find to steal, and was trying to make a name for himself. Nothing will advance your recognition or your career faster than exhibiting the ability to be tough and violent. He killed his first man at the tender age of thirteen, a member of a rival gang who had made the mistake of flirting with the girlfriend of one of Ray's bosses. Ray Martinez was now thirty-two and at least twelve more men had died by his hand. His conscience did not suffer from any violence that he might be involved in. Ray had no conscience, it had ceased to exist.

But Ray had accomplished more than just commit gross acts of violence. He had used his head and gotten himself out of the barrio: first to Chihuahua City, and then to Nuevo Casas Grandes where he climbed higher in the echelon of the Narco organization. He began crossing over into the United States, first as a mule and then as a guide; and then he had traveled as far north as Phoenix, and then Denver where he became one of the chief enforcers of the Denver narcotics underworld. But street savvy had never overlapped into knowledge of getting along in the American mainstream. He had learned a little English but not enough to sound like a citizen. He had refrained from tattooing his face and neck but still acted and looked like a Narco thug. He was extremely smart but refused to separate himself from the violent Narco culture. Eventually the authorities in Denver had put enough heat on him that he had returned to Chihuahua. For three months he had laid low in Nuevo Casas Grandes but had been called up, because of his knowledge and experience in Phoenix, to lead this expedition into the United States.

By the time the first initial round of confusion, complete with considerable cursing and pointing of fingers, was over, it was ten in the morning. The snow that had begun to fall had increased and the temperature had dropped to 30 degrees, but it had a cooling effect on the men. They decided they should attempt to get the pickup out of its bogged down state instead of abandoning it, which would mean an immediate loss of 20 percent of their product. After a cooler round of conversation, the jefe— one and the same as the pilot who had guided the truck off into the mud, although he cursed the driver profusely for his incompetence while the other men were split on who should carry the majority of blame—decided the big bosses who were safe back at the ranch south of the border should be notified of their predicament. Shift the burden of decision onto a more important individual. Especially if he was far away and couldn't get his hands on you. The patrón south of the line cursed, but his cursing was, at least for the time being, ineffective. He agreed - they should retrieve the truck out of the quagmire and save the valuable cargo. He would send help, which meant some shovels and jacks, two of them. So what? They already had jacks! They needed tow chains or ropes. They needed machinery!

Sending more vehicles north at this time was risky because their allotted slot of safety was soon to be gone: sunup until noon. But the decision had been made. It was now snowing in earnest and it was sticking to the ground, so the men got into their trucks and ran the engines and the heaters. Help was supposed to arrive before sundown.

They consumed some of the food they had packed, which wasn't much, because they had planned on being in Phoenix within twenty-four hours.

One of the men ventured downstream seeking a hiding place to facilitate a call of nature, and having walked a mere 100 yards through some thick brush, he spied what he knew was a godsend. Godsend was not a good enough word, it was a miracle. There sat a very large bulldozer. A Caterpillar D8N to be exact. Someone had been operating the big machine repairing a large earthen dam situated in a side draw that drained into the creek where their vehicle was stuck. The dozer was sitting there parked, and nobody seemed to be about. It had been hidden from their view by trees and brush, and they had failed to see the tracks the machine had made when someone had walked it to its current position. The man who found this gem was not himself an equipment operator, but he knew at least one if not two of his nine companions had some experience operating equipment. He did his business, and when finished he hurried back to tell of his find.

The word about the Caterpillar bulldozer created quite a stir among the men. The jefe had already been on the satellite radio conversing with the big bosses at the cartel's ranch twenty miles to the south, and it had been decided that a truck would be sent north within the hour with supplies and tools such as shovels. The jefe considered calling the big bosses back and telling them to wait because they now had a bulldozer at their disposal, but then he decided against the call. The truck bringing help had probably already departed and the bulldozer hadn't been started.

The jefe ordered the one that he considered his best man, Vidal, to find a high spot some distance to the south and set up a good surveillance point. Vidal set out with his rifle and a backpack containing some canned food, a phone, a satellite radio, and binoculars. The only pair available.

Vidal did not like Ray Martinez. The two had never met prior to three days before their breach of the border but had been given the opportunity to get acquainted as the team of ten men who would be sent north, two in each truck, had prepared for the expedition. Vidal considered Ray to be conceited, brash, and too full of himself with his talk of violent deeds he had committed on both sides of the line. In Vidal's opinion, the only way a caravan of this size would make it through to its destination in Phoenix was access to good intelligence and being as discreet as possible. A lot of loud talking and gunfire would get five trucks nowhere and would get them there fast. Vidal not only disliked Ray, he didn't like the mission in general. It was too big.

Several men who claimed to be experienced equipment operators were sent to retrieve the bulldozer which would end all of their troubles. Actually, there was only one man who had ever operated a dozer, and it was an old International TD25 with a cable lift, and probably fifty years old. Compared to a TD25, the D8N that they were hoping to fire up was as different as a Model A to a Rolls Royce. The Caterpillar was controlled with levers maneuvered by hand as ones' arms laid on the arm rests of the cushioned chair which sat twisted slightly to the right. It was easier to run than a car, if one knew what the buttons and levers were for.

The man who claimed to be a dozer operator looked in amazement at a pedal on the floor saying he had never seen a bulldozer with a foot-operated accelerator. Actually it was a decelerator and the throttle was a lever on the dash. He knew nothing of decelerators. He explained to his comrades that the first thing they needed to do was get the pony motor fired up and then that would be used to turn the big diesel over a revolution or two, and it would then burst into action. But neither he nor his friends could find the pony motor or a rope and pulley to get it started. It did not have a pony motor, but instead it had an electric starter like a car or pickup. About the time he figured that out, he began looking for a key or switch; and after a good deal of searching, one was finally found, and the key was even in its place. But nothing would happen when it was turned or the buttons were pushed. They decided the batteries might be dead or the terminals corroded, but they couldn't find the batteries. They were hidden behind a sheet-metal covering that would require a 5/8 inch wrench to get into. They had no wrenches. It was now two o'clock in the afternoon. They walked back to where their pickups were parked.

At three thirty in the afternoon a pickup arrived from Mexico. It had snowed for about four hours, and four or five inches had accumulated, but now it was beginning to clear off and a breeze blew. It was cold. For two hours the men dug behind the tires and under the chassis of the stuck pickup using the shovels the truck from Mexico had brought them, and then finally when they thought sufficient digging had been accomplished, a tow rope made out of nylon webbing and brought by the same truck as the shovels was attached to the rear of the stuck vehicle and the other end to the newly arrived pickup, and they tried to pull the stuck vehicle out to no avail. It would not budge even though the truck doing the pulling spun its tires and hit the end of the rope on the run.

The sun went down and it got dark, and it was time for another round of cursing and stomping of feet. The jefe started to get tough, acting mean, but the men gave him looks of disgust. He had piloted the pickup off into the muddy creek bottom, and they all knew it. They also knew that if he was going to lead them out of this predicament he would need their help. He knew he would need their help, and so he calmed down. He might need a friend in the near future, or several friends. They palavered and decided to spend the night as comfortable as possible, sleeping in the cabs of their trucks. Orders were given to only run the engines and heaters ten minutes an hour to conserve fuel.

The next morning at early light they began working, but nothing went well. For some reason the thought of unloading the dope out of the stuck truck, making it much lighter, never occurred to them. They decided they needed two trucks pulling on the disabled truck, but they had no other rope. One of the men noticed a steel cable hanging off of the windmill tower at the well, and with wrenches brought by the newly arrived truck, they managed to get the cable disconnected from the well, and they used that to hook a second pickup up to the stuck truck. They revved their engines and spun the tires but to no avail. The jefe got mad again and had a cursing fit. He screamed at the men driving the tow trucks, telling them to hit the stuck truck more violently. They did and a bumper was jerked off of the latest truck that had come from Mexico. More cursing.

The jefe had several long conversations with his bosses in Mexico who offered suggestions. Mostly the men dug with the shovels, and they also used wrenches to finish taking the damaged bumper off of the pickup and nothing worked. Two men were sent with wrenches to try a second time to get the bulldozer started. With wrenches they took the steel plate off that hid the batteries, and using a wrench they arced battery terminals across each other and created sparks. Convinced the batteries were charged, they began undoing wiring they thought they could reroute and jumpstart the engine. Nothing they did went well. Finally, after a considerable amount of molesting to important electrical wires, they gave up. Leaving the batteries uncovered, they walked back to their companions.

After a long cold and bitter day, they were beat. Over the radio the jefe learned that someone in the United States had been contacted, and they could be assured that they would go undetected for another twenty-four hours. They were sending more help tomorrow. The jefe argued and said they needed to start moving the next day, and if that meant leaving one pickup load behind, they would do so. They needed to get going. The men were running out of food. Was there any talk of sending more? No one knew. It was cold. Was there talk of blankets? No. But the jefe decided tomorrow they were proceeding north, one way or the other.

The next morning, a full forty-eight hours after leaving Mexico, the Mexican men, who now numbered twelve, awoke to clear skies and 18 degrees. Another truck having someone with new ideas was supposed to arrive by 9:00 a.m. They were restless and related their acute dissatisfaction to the jefe. And then at eight o'clock, Vidal, who had positioned himself on a hill a mile to the south, called the jefe on the satellite radio. A lone white pickup was approaching, and he did not think it was friendly. It was still several miles away, but he felt certain it was coming toward them.

Hurriedly, the jefe sent five men with the truck lately arrived out of Mexico to backtrack on the road and try to conceal it and themselves in a side canyon or somewhere.

He ordered them to let the pickup pass them if it came their way. He ordered the other men to take the remaining trucks and drive them behind some of the trees and brush that lay between them and the bulldozer and hide. They knew what to do. They had radios. They would stay in touch and would react according to how it played out.

Chapter Two
January 7, 2016
Morning

The Cloverdale Road left the small community of
Animas and went straight south. After forty-two
miles it reached Cloverdale, which was a ghost town that
never did amount to anything more than half a dozen
buildings and maybe twice that many residents. But at
least the ghost town had a road named after it.

The lion's share of the Cloverdale Road passed
through one of America's largest cattle ranches, the
legendary Las Animas, which stretched over a million
acres of the Chihuahuan Desert. Animas Peak rose up
in the center of the ranch and the Continental Divide
separated the ranch's east side from its west. The
Continental Divide surrounding Animas Peak was
the spot where the West's most celebrated hunter, Ben
Lilly, first walked into New Mexico coming north out
of Mexico where he had spent several years living off
of the land, killing mountain lions and bears that were
preying upon the peons' livestock, and hiding out from
encroaching civilization. Ben Lilly was the man who
killed the last grizzly bear in Hidalgo County on the
very slopes of Animas Peak itself. By killing the bear he
destroyed his reason for being there, and so he traveled
north to the Mogollon Mountains.

But Animas Peak was still there with Las Animas Ranch sprawling in all directions from its peak. In many ways the country in those parts was no tamer than when Ben Lilly was there, and cowboys on fast horses still rounded up cattle in the old tradition with that being about the only way to make a living there. Cowboying, the taking care of cattle.

Ben Moody and his wife, Caroline, lived south of Animas a mile or so on the Cloverdale Road. Ben had a few sections of country leased, and he laid claim to a small herd of beef cows. At least the Western Bank in Lordsburg, thirty-five miles to the north, allowed him to claim them as Ben successfully made his payments. Ben loved his cows and having his brand on fifty cows was a thing of pride to him. To Caroline they were sometimes a burden. She wondered why a man would work himself to the bone and sacrifice the things that most modern American males pursued—expensive boats, motorhomes, fast cars and a tract home in a cul-de-sac—for a bunch of starving cows. She wondered why people like her husband tried to raise calves on the drought-stricken Chihuahuan Desert. Mostly she wished that Ben didn't have to work so hard to make ends meet. She loved her man. She didn't need Tammy Wynette to preach to her about sticking by her man. At times she got sick of his starving cows that required so much attention, but she never got tired of him.

To supplement the income that the fifty starving cows produced, Ben Moody worked for a local legend named Tommy Davis who owned some heavy equipment such as a couple of bulldozers and backhoes, a road grader, a loader, and a dump truck. Tommy could and would do any kind of dirt work: build roads, blade roads, put in septic systems, and build or maintain earthen dams that were used to water cattle on ranches. Tommy had been around forever and his father before him. He had the unusual quality of being well liked and respected by everyone, probably because he was a man who could get things done. If you wanted a mountain moved, Tommy Davis could do it; and he was always fair with everyone. He didn't lie and he never overcharged for his work. His word was his bond.

Ben Moody ran equipment for Tommy Davis, and sometimes he performed mechanic work when needed. A great deal of their work was for the sprawling Las Animas Ranch where there was always a stock pond that needed fixed or a road bladed or any number of other dirt work that might be requested by the wealthy ranch owner.

On this particular day, a Thursday, Ben rose early and enjoyed his usual breakfast and coffee with Caroline. He could not recall any morning in their thirty years of marriage when she had not risen up early and cooked him breakfast. It was and always had been their special time together. They had four children, all of them grown and gone, although not far away. They all got along. Ben was a very soft spoken man and never a fighter. He shunned away from fighting. No one in his family could remember him ever raising his voice or talking ill of anyone, even someone that he didn't like. Oddly, old Tommy Davis, who was twenty years Ben's senior, was the same way; so the saying opposites attract wasn't necessarily true in this case. Between the two of them, Tommy and Ben, they sort of purred ahead like a diesel engine, getting their work done at a steady pace. They were the epitome of the word dependable.

At 7:00 a.m. sharp, Ben left the house that he and Caroline shared south of Animas and on the west side of the Cloverdale Road. He had to go south and onto the Las Animas Ranch and fix the Caterpillar D8N bulldozer that he had left parked by a dirt tank that he had cleaned the mud out of near Birch Springs. The dozer had blown an electrical relay in the wiring going to the starter, and the part had finally arrived after a week of waiting; and he planned to replace the relay, a process that would take him ten minutes. He drove away from his ranchito in a 4-wheel drive pickup that had a utility bed on the back instead of the traditional pickup bed. In the various compartments of the toolbox, there was in the vicinity of $10,000 worth of tools, most of which belonged to him.

He pulled out onto the Cloverdale Road and turned right. At this point the road was paved with asphalt and was that way for fifteen miles or so. After going about fourteen miles, he passed the XT Camp, one of many cow camps on the sprawling Las Animas outfit. At the same point where the Cloverdale Road passed the XT another road, a slightly improved dirt one, left the Cloverdale Road going off to the southeast toward Adobe Creek and another cow camp known as the Adobes. Married cowboys worked and lived at both of these cow camps. Both of these cowboys and their wives were friends of Ben's.

The road going to the Adobes continued on to the southeast after passing that juncture and went to an old ranch known as the OK Bar, but it was deserted. At the OK Bar the road found itself in a deep canyon with Animas Peak itself looming up to the southwest about three and a half miles away and 3,000 feet higher. From the OK Bar the country began to get wilder and rougher in all directions especially to the south toward the Lynch Camp, eleven miles away, or the well at Birch Springs seven miles away. But the roads in the area were very rocky and in some places very steep and seldom used.

So Ben continued south on the Cloverdale Road that led peacefully down the bottom of the Animas Valley on Animas Peak's west side.

As he passed the XT Camp, Ben noticed the Border Patrol's MSC unit, a portable ground radar system mounted on the flat bed of a large dually Ford truck. The radar unit could, according to the Border Patrol, pick up and track moving objects on the ground up to seven miles away. Moving things like animals, deer, antelope, or human beings, or moving vehicles. From the vantage point where the radar unit had been parked for weeks the man at the controls could see down the country toward the Adobes Camp and the OK Bar, which was and had been a major thoroughfare for Mexican drug smugglers known as mules. A mule train of ten guys with each man having a 50-pound pack on his back could transport 500 pounds of marijuana north, and if the correct intelligence had been provided by scouts and cooperating American citizens as to the whereabouts of the Border Patrol or other law enforcement, the ten-man mule train could move the contraband up to twenty miles a day. It happened all the time.

Ben continued on south on the Cloverdale Road, and several miles south of the XT Camp and the Adobes turnoff, he passed a road going to the west and leading to a Border Patrol forward operating base that was an extension of the Lordsburg Border Patrol Station where about 200 agents were stationed. Three to six of these agents stayed at the forward operation base (F.O.B.) for several days at a time. The idea behind these F.O.B.s was to deploy agents closer to the border so they would not have so much of their eight-hour shift taken up driving, if indeed they were sent to the border from the Lordsburg station which was at the closest point seventy-five miles north of the international boundary. Actually, on any given day, 90 percent of the Lordsburg Border Patrol assets were deployed somewhere in the northern half of Hidalgo County. By all appearances to any casual observer, the real border seemed to be Highway 9 which went east to west, beginning at Santa Teresa and going west to Columbus, and then Hachita and then Animas. At Animas and Hachita Highway 9 was close to fifty miles north of the border.

Ben kept driving, and about sixteen miles south of the XT, he passed Las Animas Ranch headquarters that lay in the bottom of the Animas Valley and five miles southwest of Animas Peak luring above it in the clouds.

There was a considerable amount of controversy and rumors based on bad information about Las Animas Ranch and its policies concerning border security. The violence and crime that the residents of the Bootheel of New Mexico (Hidalgo County) as well as Cochise County, Arizona, directly to the west, had experienced for twenty years was painful to all who had lived through it. Mexican Narcos traveling north with dope on their backs would return, and on their way south, they had burglarized, vandalized, and committed murder. Virtually everyone who was a permanent resident of the area had been affected. To the residents in the back-wood, rural areas, seeing alien traffic was a daily occurrence.

As a result of this illegal activity and the stress put on American citizens in the area, there had been many town hall or community-type meetings produced where civilians and law enforcement personnel and/or politicians, many of them famous and wanting to make hay over the situation, would discuss, make speeches, scream, holler, point fingers, and curse at each other for the lack of security the U.S. government was providing its citizens. Occasionally something productive would result from these meetings, but, for the most part, people thought they were a dog-and-pony show. The Border Patrol had a long history of doing what it wanted regardless of what some angry rancher or dumb-ass politician might scream or holler about.

The owners of Las Animas Ranch had locked several gates going into several large pastures because of the destruction of roads, fences, and waterlines resulting from Border Patrol agents driving too fast and irresponsibly - so the ranch owners had said. Some people, especially several rural residents of Cochise County who were always at the meetings, began speaking out at these various meetings accusing Las Animas Ranch of denying the Border Patrol access to the border. This wasn't true. The border itself and the Roosevelt Easement, which was a sixty-foot-wide area running from coast to coast and adjacent to the border on the north side, had not been locked off. There were no pastures anywhere on Las Animas Ranch where Border Patrol agents were not welcomed on foot. The Border Patrol's special horse patrol had access to every inch of Las Animas Ranch, and the ranch encouraged and welcomed the use of horses to patrol the area. Also no one, not even the owner of Las Animas Ranch, could control the sky and deny a Department of Homeland Security helicopter from searching the ground from the air or landing and letting Border Patrol agents out of the aircraft and setting them loose to pursue alien traffic.

It was obvious that most of the bad remarks about Las Animas Ranch and its owners were a result of jealousy and bad intelligence. The Border Patrol could get to the border anytime it wanted. That was the problem, it preferred patrolling Highway 9, fifty miles to the north and liked Interstate 10, twenty miles farther, that much better.

Ben Moody had contemplated all of these things thoroughly and held strong opinions about them. All aspects of the border security problem interested him because, like all residents of the area, he had been affected by the massive onslaught of smuggling and illegal immigration. But interested as he may have been, he had not got involved in the politics. He was not a speech maker or an activist. He hated meetings and shunned the spotlight. He made it a habit of letting law enforcement and politicians deal with the problem, which he felt was their duty and calling. He personally did his best to ignore alien traffic, which was, in his opinion, the only way to keep one's sanity. It was a problem far too big for a cowboy to deal with in his opinion. He left the outlaw Mexicans alone, and he hoped they would leave him alone.

When he had traveled seven miles south of Las Animas Ranch headquarters, he left the Cloverdale Road and turned east toward San Luis Pass which was another seven miles distance. As he drove he encountered no Border Patrol vehicles or Las Animas Ranch cowboys. He saw no one. After traversing the Continental Divide and San Luis Pass, he drove a couple miles and then turned north toward the Lynch Camp. There were still patches of snow on the ground with the ground being about 70 percent covered by an inch or two of the white stuff. He noticed the tracks of a vehicle that had passed this way some time since the snow had fallen. He wondered who had made the tracks and decided it must have been a Border Patrol vehicle. When he came to the new road that he had made with the Caterpillar dozer only a few days before he turned left and noticed the same tracks leading that way in the snow.

About a mile from Birch Springs, the road began a descent down a side canyon, and it became more winding and steep as it went. The thickness and density of the brush and trees increased, which at times made the road somewhat like a tunnel or channel through a mountain. At times visibility was close to zero, except for the few feet between his position and the next curve in the road. And then finally the path broke out into the openness of the shallow canyon that the Birch Springs Well lay in.

When the road hit the canyon floor he turned sharply to the right, toward the direction of the bulldozer a quarter mile away, and that was when he saw it: a red 3/4 ton Chevrolet pickup resting in the bottom of the creek bed. It was eerie how even at several hundred yards distance, the truck had a disabled look to it. He instantly saw and recognized the bales of dope loaded in the pickup bed as well as a few that had been unloaded and strewn about. He saw the tracks that had been left by someone's massive effort at dislodging the truck from its moorings. Immediately he stopped his truck. Staring from the distance at the sight that lay before him, he understood without being told what had taken place. He recognized failure. Failure of a mission. He had a sick feeling in his stomach of its implications. "Oh hell! Here we go again!" He spoke the words out loud. He turned his Ford pickup around and started backtracking out of Birch Springs Canyon. He had seen all of this he wanted to see.

Chapter Three
January 7, 2016
10:00 a.m.

Ben Moody turned his Ford pickup around and started out of the Birch Springs Canyon, backtracking himself up the narrow and winding road that ascended the little tributary. He had done a great deal of work on this road with the big D8N dozer only ten days earlier, there having been a faint two-track road there before which had been washed out with decades of flood water coming from occasional rains. Even though it had received his recent attention it was still a tight, winding, and very rocky road; and it was slow going. His mind was full of questions about the truck loaded with dope and where its occupants might have disappeared to.

He had gone perhaps 300 yards and was still in the bottom of the narrow side canyon when he caught a brief glimpse of a white vehicle coming toward him. At that particular spot, the juniper and other types of brush grew very dense and close to the road, which restricted the possibility of any long range vision, with the exception of looking straight up. His first thought was that the approaching vehicle must be a Border Patrol agent driving the usual white vehicle with a green stripe running downward between the door of the cab and the rear of the vehicle. Almost immediately he found a wide spot in the road on his right side, affording him room to pull over and stop and give the approaching vehicle room to get by. He stopped and waited.

There was a sharp corner in the canyon road immediately ahead of him less the seventy feet away, and within several seconds of Ben's getting stopped in the wide spot, a white Chevy pickup came rambling around the corner. At first he was confused because he was expecting a Border Patrol agent, but instead he saw two men riding on the hood of the truck, directly over the engine. They were dressed in full camouflage fatigues and coats and had camouflage-colored netted hoods over their entire heads, the type a hunter would buy at Cabelas or some other hunting supply store.

The truck approached fast and ran directly up to the Ranch Hand grill guard attached to the front of Ben's Ford truck. This move put an end to any possibility of forward movement coming from Ben's truck. Things began to happen with lightning speed. The men on the hood of the Chevy slid off and moved swiftly toward him, two of them coming to the right side, or passenger side, of the truck.

Doors flew open on the Mexican's truck, and several men jumped out and ran toward him, coming up to the driver's window. Ben had rolled his window down. "Get out!" A Mexican man told him in broken English from the outside of Ben's pickup door.

"No, you guys leave me alone. I'm not bothering you. I just want to go on. I haven't seen anything!"

"No, you get out. We need your truck. Get out!"

"No, I'm not going to get out. I haven't seen anything! I'm just going to go on and mind my own business." Ben was aware that the men who had run to the right side of his truck had opened the passenger-side door and were searching the interior of his truck. Their hands were inches away from his belt. They had found his lunch box and were going through his things. They began eating his lunch, even as he was arguing with the masked man out the driver's side door.

"Get out of your truck. We need your truck." The man doing all of the talking got ahold of the door handle and jerked the door open, and now there were five men, three on the driver's side and two on the passenger's side. A man on the left side of the truck reached in and grabbed Ben and began dragging him out. In a last desperate act, he got ahold of the pistol grip of a 5-shot, .38 Special double action revolver that he kept partly concealed by shoving the barrel down between the driver's seat and the console in the middle of the front seat. As he was being drug out of the truck by the Mexican doing most of the talking, he came up with his pistol with the intention of sticking it in the Mexican's face, and then the Mexicans saw it.

"Pistola! Pistola! Pistola!" they shouted in Spanish, and Ben saw one of the men pulling out a semi-automatic pistol and pointing it at his head.

Swiftly, several of his captors had their hands on him, and he realized he had no chance of fighting so he allowed them to take his pistol away from him. They pushed him down to the ground with his face and knees both touching the rocky ground and his waist remaining up. As they mashed on him, his brain recognized that at least one of the men was talking on a radio in code talk, while others cursed him for not cooperating. For a few moments Ben experienced feelings of sheer, overpowering terror, and then as the Mexicans realized that he had ceased to be a threat they became calmer, and they brought him back up to a standing position. They tried to pull his hands behind his back and tie them, but because of arthritis and stiffness from old injuries, they couldn't get his hands close enough to tie so they brought them around in front and tied them together. While standing erect, he was searched thoroughly for more weapons, but nothing was found that alarmed them.

The initial excitement of Ben's capture settled down somewhat after they got him back on his feet and tied his hands. They knew they had him and had successfully compromised his ability to fight, so they began to act more businesslike. One of the men had found Ben's wallet in his lunch box, and from that they found his identification and also retrieved the registration out of the truck's console. Armed with this information, they started talking on a satellite radio. Ben listened intently but could not make much sense of any information being forwarded through the airwaves other than his name and address, the license plate number off of the truck, as well as Tommy Davis' name and address which was on the truck's registration.

The dialogue he overheard was partly in Spanish and partly in broken English with a variety of military sounding code words which included the use of numbers and some odd sounding Mexican slang, or that was what Ben perceived it to be. He could understand nothing but he and his employer's names and was convinced in his own mind that the words being used were a well-defined code language designed to baffle anyone who might be secretly listening.

At no time during this period did Ben get to look at any of the men's faces because they were all covered, several with the hunters' hoods earlier described and several with knitted stocking caps complete with holes for the wearer's eyes. One man had on a turban made of material wrapped spirally from the top of his head going downward, and the end of it kept wrapping around the man's face. It reminded Ben of something you might see in the Middle East, but he had no idea if the man who wore it was from that part of the world nor could he tell if the headpiece had any religious significance. Ben had seen illegal aliens that had been captured by the Border Patrol that he was told were from India, and their headgear had been similar. The Border Patrol called these people, as well as all aliens that originate somewhere besides Mexico, OTMs (other than Mexican). Was this man an OTM? He had no idea, but he did feel that, after watching the man's actions, he was special. He seemed to be the guard, always looking off in the distance and occupied with a duty other than taking part with the others in their dealings with him.

Ben kept telling the men, "Let me go; I won't say anything to anyone. I'll walk to Animas, and that will take me at least twelve hours, and you can be long gone by then. You can have my truck."

And the Mexicans repeatedly answered him saying, "No, it's too dangerous." That made Ben wonder - dangerous for whom?

His body was shaking and the Mexicans asked him, "Why are you shaking?"

"Well, I'm scared for one thing, and for another I'm colder than heck. My coat's in my pickup and it's cold out here. If something happens to me, what's going to happen to my family? My family will suffer!"

It seemed to Ben that one of the men who had been holding him acted kinder than the others. He retrieved Ben's coat out of the cab of his truck, and they momentarily untied him and let him put the coat on. "You are going to stay with us today. Later, we will turn you loose."

Then there was more code talk on the radio with someone off in the distance. The men seemed to be following orders. They got some kind of big rag and wrapped Ben's head with it to blindfold him and then began pushing him toward the back of his truck. The ground was very rocky, and Ben stumbled in the rocks because of not being able to see, and they started acting as if they were pissed off. They shoved him through the rocks, and he stumbled worse and fell forward slamming his head into a toolbox on the side of his utility bed on the back of his truck. The men cursed him, "Lo siento viejo bastardo." When they reached the back of the truck, Ben sensed that they wanted him to climb up into the bed between the toolboxes, but he couldn't negotiate this task with his hands tied. They cursed him some more and then picked him up and threw him into the truck.

Immediately they were moving with Ben being jostled about among various tools and toolboxes. He was aware that at least one person was in the back of the truck with him. After a short ride they stopped the truck, and Ben was unloaded and then led by the hand a ways and told to sit down on a large rock. One man was left with him as a guard, and every time Ben would make any kind of a move, even something as insignificant as scratching his nose or repositioning himself on the rock, the guard would tell him, "No, no, no, don't try to do anything!"

"I'm not trying to do anything." He could tell they had gone back down to the creek near Birch Springs, and the men were working at getting the truck out of its stuck position in the creek bed. He was offered something to eat and accepted a sandwich, but then, because of his nervous state of mind, he was unable to eat it.

All afternoon Ben could hear vehicles coming and going. He could recognize the different sounds coming from different vehicles, some of them being very quiet while others were loud. Some of them rattled and banged like something wore-out, while others sounded new. He had the impression that there were lots of vehicles. There were also lots of voices, some of which he could hear plainly, and they were speaking Spanish, but he knew they were not Mexican: Like anyone who had lived a lifetime near the Mexican border, Ben knew the sound of a true Spanish-speaking Mexican, and there were people talking who absolutely did not have the brogue.

After several hours the jefe came over to him and said, "Where is your wench?"

"I don't have a wench."

The jefe hit Ben in the back of his head. Because the punch was unseen and unexpected, it about knocked Ben off of his rock. "Where's your wench?" the jefe demanded, this time loud and angry.

"I don't have a wench! I've got a come-along in my truck, but I don't have a wench." The jefe slapped the back of his head again and then walked away cursing.

After a while the jefe returned and asked, "When will someone be expecting you in?"

"Well," Ben paused, "around three thirty to five."

This made the jefe angry and he slapped Ben again, "Which is it, three thirty or five?"

"Well, we come in at all times of day or night, but let's say five."

The jefe walked away.

Ben asked permission to pee, and the guard gave him permission, so he stood up and relieved himself.

By catching glimpses of daylight and slight bits of scenery through the cracks between his face and the blindfold, Ben could tell it was still daylight but getting toward dusk. About this time the men began arguing and cursing and seemed to be fighting amongst themselves. Code talk, cryptic messaging, and the voices of what he thought were gringos trying to sound like Mexicans seemed to increase. There was more traffic. Tension seemed to flow through the air like electricity. Ben became more nervous and worried about his own life and that of his family. He couldn't imagine why it would be so difficult for this many men to get a truck unstuck and pulled out of the mud. He remembered the men telling him that they couldn't turn him loose because it was too dangerous. Was something going on right now that was dangerous?

One man, whose voice Ben could recognize, had come and talked to him several times throughout the day, and the man's voice seemed kinder, much kinder than the jefe's. The man had asked him, "Are you alright?" and "Why are you shaking?"

"I'm worried about my family."

"Don't do anything foolish and you will be all right."

It got dark, and Ben considered running, but he knew that he was somewhat crippled like many working men his age, and he figured that he wouldn't get far; and then there would really be hell-to-pay when they caught him.

After it had been dark a little while, someone came and got him, and they led him to a truck, but he had no idea which one. When they reached the truck, a door was opened for him, and he was pushed in. He sat in the passenger's seat, but after a second he was punched in the head and ribs, and a man grunted pushing him toward the middle. He had to be helped up, because they had stacked small marijuana bricks on the seat in the middle. They wanted him to sit on top of the bricks, which he did, but this made him so tall that his face was pushed up against the ceiling of the cab of the truck. "Let me go." Ben pleaded.

"Shut up!" the jefe who sat next to him replied, and the truck moved forward.

They drove for what Ben felt like was a long way, all the while him being very uncomfortable with his face in the ceiling; and then suddenly they stopped, and Ben could hear more hollering and confusion. He was told to get out, which was a relief. They led him to the front of the truck he had been riding in, and they took his blindfold off. They had been driving with no lights and it was very dark. He was aware that there were several trucks and more men than the two which he had been riding with, but he could not ascertain how many. "Where are we? You are going to show us how to get to Animas," the jefe demanded.

Ben looked around. The night sky was pitch black. He had been riding on top of bricks of dope with his face rubbing into the ceiling of a pickup, and now he was supposed to look off into the abyss and tell his captors where they were and where they were going. And then, before he could fabricate an answer, the Narcos, the jefe himself, said, "We are going back to Mexico, when we get to a main road we will let you go." This ludicrous statement really confused Ben. Only seconds earlier the man had instructed him to take them to Animas (north), and now the jefe announced they were going to return to Mexico. Because of the statement about Mexico, Ben thought they were pointed south but they were in fact pointed east, but it was all irrelevant because gazing into the black night in his stressed-out state of mind, Ben had no idea where they were. He told the Narcos just that, and the jefe became angry. But then they admitted that they had taken a side road that showed up on the jefe's infamous topographical map, and they had run into a bad washout that made the road completely impassable.

As a result of Ben's inability to explain where they were, and the jefe having to admit that he was responsible for getting them lost, they all loaded back up and backtracked to Birch Springs and their starting point. It didn't take as long as Ben thought it would. Being blindfolded distorted everything, including time. Now they left the blindfold off, but Ben was not allowed to look down to where the truck was stuck.

When they arrived back at Birch Springs, Ray Martinez, the jefe, got out his topographical map and studied it. Showing the map to Ben, he pointed to a road that left Birch Springs going west and eventually turning north after it crossed over to the west side of the Continental Divide. Ben knew the road to be an old abandoned wagon road that had probably been washed out for fifty years or longer. In response to the jefe's questioning look, Ben said, "No bueno." This response sent the jefe into a rage and he slapped the paper map against the dash of the truck. "Mentiroso hijo de puta ¿ porqué sigues problemas?"

Remaining in the rage, the jefe got out and told two men from another truck to walk to the west and try to find the road that he so wanted to be there. After fifteen minutes they came back and reported finding no evidence of a road.

By then the moon had risen over the horizon and created enough light to make driving with no headlights much easier and faster. The caravan of drug-laden trucks left Birch Springs going south on the road they all had come in on in the beginning of this odyssey. Ben did not know the exact number of trucks there were, but he was aware that it was more than just two or three. He wondered how many times that some of them had been up and down this part of the road while he sat blindfolded listening to numerous vehicles coming and going.

After going several miles they came to an earthen dam and pond (referred to by cowboys in the southwest as a dirt tank) called the Pit. There was a crossroads there, and they turned east and after several miles came to another dirt tank known as the T9. In the moonlight Ben could recognize the country and knew they were headed toward Deer Creek and the Deer Creek Road, which would, if passable, take them on north to the Spur Tank, the Frankie, and eventually the canyon at the head of Adobe Creek, the OK Bar, the Adobes Camp Road and the Cloverdale Road.

As they passed the T9, Ben knew that using the Deer Creek Road and the route just mentioned there was about twenty miles of rough going before they would reach the Cloverdale Road. He had not been on this route in several years and doubted that much of anybody had, and he wondered if they would be able to negotiate the route with the overloaded trucks. They rose up on the divide between the Adobe Creek drainage that flowed north and the Deer Creek drainage that flowed south. They were between the Spur and the Frankie, and the road became impossible to see in places due to tall grass. Several times men got out and walked afoot looking for the road. Then they came to a place where the road and surrounding countryside fell off at a steep angle, and the road looked dangerous. The jefe wanted Ben to get them to Animas, but Ben knew in his own mind that he wouldn't want to drive his own truck down off of that slope, especially not being sure that the road might be even worse just a mile or two ahead. It was simply too wild and remote a country to be driving around in overloaded vehicles. But did he dare tell the jefe he shouldn't proceed? He was afraid the Mexican might finally lose all control of his anger and frustration and really start beating on him or worse. The Mexican boss was acting high, and Ben was sure he had started ingesting some form of narcotic but did not know what exactly it was.

Suddenly, as they peered off into the darkness and the canyon created by the headwaters of Adobe Creek, one of the Mexican's radios went off, and that created much cryptic conversation between the Mexicans. The mood changed to acute nervousness, and Ben realized that this excitement created by the newly arrived message coming from the radio had taken away any opportunity or responsibility he might have had concerning forward movement. The caravan was going to continue north and off into the abyss, whether he liked it or not. They baled off the rocky slope with abandonment, and it seemed to Ben that they had passed the point of no return. Ben had not been blindfolded for several hours due to the fact that the jefe needed his guidance, and he looked at his watch and noticed it was 11:00 p.m.

Chapter Four
January 7, 2016
6:00 p.m.

The sun went down on the Moody ranchito at about a quarter past five, and Ben Moody had not returned home. Not getting home on time wasn't a thing that was unheard of, but to Caroline sundown was an event that was noticed. Actually, Ben had told her that morning he would probably be home in the early afternoon because the repair job he was planning on performing on the Caterpillar bulldozer was not a complicated or time-consuming task. He had already made plans with Tommy Davis to return the following day, January 8, to start walking the big piece of machinery to a different site a few miles away. Tommy, or maybe his son-in-law, Chester Franks, would go with Ben and drive his pickup while Ben drove the bulldozer. Ben had also talked to Caroline about going with him to drive his truck while he moved the dozer, but they had not finalized that decision. But on this day, Thursday the 7th, Ben had no plans on doing anything but fixing the dozer and returning home. He had hopes of checking on his cows before sundown; a thing that he enjoyed doing and did as often as possible.

As the sun disappeared, Caroline wondered why her man wasn't home. He had been so sure of returning early. She watched the minutes click by on the clock hanging on the kitchen wall, and every five minutes she got up and looked out the window. By six it was pitch black outside, and she saw no lights coming. From the kitchen window she could see down the Cloverdale Road for about five miles, and several times she saw lights coming north, but then when they got to the turnoff to their place they proceeded on north.

At 6:15 Caroline called Tommy Davis who, with his wife Betty, lived five miles to the east on a ranch that had been in Tommy's family for a century. "Hello," Betty Davis said on the other end.

"Betty, this is Caroline. Ben is not home yet, and I was expecting him early, like one or two, but he's still not here. Has Tommy said anything to you about some change of plans?"

"Thomas," Betty said rather loudly, "Ben has not returned home yet, you better come and talk to Caroline."

"Hello Carol." Tommy had picked up the phone. "You say Ben isn't home yet?"

"No, sir, he's not."

"Well, I'll be a son of a gun. I thought he was just going down to Birch Springs and rewire that dozer. Did he say anything to you about doin' somethin' else?"

"No sir. He told me the same thing. Said he would be home early." She looked out her kitchen window again but saw no headlights.

"Well, I'll be a son of a gun, he shoulda been back by now. Maybe that old Ford truck finally quit him. I'll tell you what, I'll call Cody Sawyer at the Fitzpatrick and see if he can drive over there to Birch Springs and find him."

"Thank you, Tommy."

"You bet, Caroline. Don't you worry, we'll go to lookin' around."

Cody Sawyer was an employee of Las Animas Ranch and close friends with both Tommy and Ben. He lived in a cow camp known as the Fitzpatrick that lay seven or eight miles west of the San Luis Pass and about forty-seven miles closer to Birch Springs than Tommy Davis. Like Tommy, he had a good radio that would enable them to communicate with each other in a lot of places where their cell phones wouldn't work. When Tommy called him on the land line and told him about the situation, he replied that, yes, he could and would drive to Birch Springs and look for Ben Moody. He would take his cell phone and his radio and would report back as soon as possible. It was about a quarter to seven when Cody Sawyer got in his truck and headed east toward Birch Springs that, by the dirt road he would travel on, was about eighteen miles to the east by northeast.

When Cody got to the turnoff east of San Luis Pass that led north toward Birch Springs, he noticed multiple pickup tracks in the snow and mud, more tracks than he would have expected to see. He had seen very little Border Patrol activity in the last several days, but perhaps they had been out making more tracks than he realized. He went north and then turned west on the newly created road that Ben Moody had plowed out of the rocky Chihuahua Desert landscape only a few days before. Again he noticed more tracks than he would have anticipated. As he drove down the last canyon that dropped into Birch Springs he noticed where several vehicles had turned around in a narrow space afforded by the tight walls of the canyon and the vegetation that hugged close to the crude roadbed. "Border Patrol must really be after something," he muttered to himself.

He followed the road down to the Birch Springs Well and then turned downstream, and in his headlights he saw what appeared to be a pickup sitting in the creek bed several hundred yards below the well. He also saw an odd array of articles scattered about all over the ground. At first, Cody couldn't tell what it all was. He drove closer and saw tracks deep enough to be called ruts that had been gouged into the soil recently made wet from the snow that had fallen several days earlier. The mud and what snow that was left was now frozen hard from the cold night air, and the ruts made Cody's vehicle bounce and lurch, and he finally stopped in the middle of what was obvious mayhem. He recognized that the stuff he saw laying around were tools, mechanic's tools, scattered over what was probably an acre of land in the canyon bottom. There were wrenches, some of them small, and others large like a 36-inch Stilson pipe wrench which lay with its handle sticking out of a windrow of mud made by the tire of a heavy truck. There were bottle jacks and boxes of large half-inch drive sockets and ratchets and electric hand-held grinders and hammers and crowbars. "What the hell?" he said to himself.

Cody got out and walked around with a flashlight looking at the various things that were strewn about, almost as if the whole scene had been orchestrated for some demonstration. He saw a black book laying on the ground, a book like a day planner, and when he picked it up he saw by the light of his flashlight that the book was Ben Moody's day planner or schedule book. His name was in it. His plans for the next several days were in it. Suddenly a cold chill came over Cody Sawyer's back. "This isn't good. No, this isn't good at all. Ben Moody's life is in this book, and he isn't here anymore." He looked off in the distance and saw papers blowing in the cold night breeze. He went and picked the papers up and saw in the light of the flashlight that the papers held some plans and diagrams of some project that someone was designing. The handwriting on these papers matched the ones in the day planner. Cody shined his powerful flashlight off in every direction looking for a person or vehicle or some sign of something that might have witnessed the scattering of the tools and the making of all the deep tracks and utter chaos that was now freezing on the January air. He saw nothing. No witnesses and no explanation. "Where in the hell is Ben Moody?" Cody said to himself.

Suddenly and unexpectedly Cody Sawyer didn't want to be in this place any longer. He was not a man that was easily frightened or nervous, but he decided that he wanted out of this hole. He got in his pickup truck and headed out the way he had come in, and when he reached the top of the ridge a mile south of Birch Springs he stopped at a place where his radio would work. It was now 8:15 in the evening.

Chapter Five
January 7, 2016
10:00 p.m.

Tommy Davis looked around the scene at Birch Springs where the Narcos' Chevy pickup sat like a sunken battleship in the creek bottom several hundred yards below the Birch Springs Well. The truck had sunk so low into the mud and sand that the pickup bed was even with the ground. It was obvious to anyone looking that someone, no doubt several people, had moved massive amounts of dirt, rock, and mud by hand using shovels in an attempt to dig the pickup out, but they had failed miserably. Behind the pickup on the side of the creek bed where the pickup had made its approach, several sets of deep cuts had been left behind, scarring the earth as one attempt after another had been made to yank the truck backwards and out of its moorings. Tools had been scattered over a large piece of the landscape, and Tommy was observant enough to realize that they had been laid out in an odd but deliberate pattern with one tool prescribed for every five yard square of available space. He observed this and wondered why the tools weren't just thrown out in a pile close to each other. Why had the people doing this packed tools around and scattered them over what Tommy thought was several acres? He walked around looking at the man-made mess and picked up and examined several tools, and recognizing them, he knew for certain they had come out of Ben's truck. Tommy and a man named Junior, another loyal employee, walked around looking for something, but not knowing what. They were looking for some kind of clue to help them understand what had taken place. Tommy found several fragments of burlap material, shredded and torn fragments about four or five inches square. Pieces of burlap that had obviously been torn off of a larger piece. He contemplated the burlap and knew that bales of marijuana were always wrapped in burlap.

"What do you think went on here, Junior?"

"Man, this is crazy! A pickup stuck in the mud, it's pretty obvious they tried to dig it out, and then they tried to pull it out. Ben's tools are scattered around over half the whole damn outfit and then Ben's truck is gone. Where's Ben? Why did he leave his tools scattered all over creation? Ben took care of his stuff, I mean, like it's crazy! I don't have it figured out."

"Look at this." Tommy showed Junior the piece of torn burlap. "What does that remind you of?"

"It's like a piece of a feed sack or something, only they don't put cow feed or horse feed in burlap sacks anymore, they use paper sacks."

"Yeah, what do they wrap in burlap now days?"

"Nothing that I know of except dope." Junior stopped and looked at Tommy and then started, "You think . . ."

Tommy interrupted, "I don't know what to think, but I will tell you one thing for sure, Ben Moody sure as hell isn't hauling drugs, but maybe he ran onto someone who was, or maybe he ran into something he wasn't supposed to. I don't know, but we know he was here and his truck was here and now it's gone. Maybe he's gone. There's some sons of bitches out there somewhere who know,

Ed Ashurst

and we need to find them. You go over there, Junior, out in front of that stuck pickup, and see if you can see any tracks going north on that old road. I am going to walk over and look around the dozer."

They parted company, and Tommy walked through the brush to the bulldozer. He realized that he and Junior could be in mortal danger with someone hiding in the dark watching them. He forced himself forward with resolve, determined to find out what happened to Ben Moody. At the dozer he found nothing, except the metal hood that covered the batteries, had been removed and was now lying on the ground as if thrown there carelessly. He knew that Ben would not have done that. He saw electrical wiring that had been molested and he knew Ben had not done that either. He walked back to his pickup where Junior was waiting.

As he walked his mind was deducing the events that had taken place since Ben had arrived. He knew that Ben had been here because he recognized the tools. Cody Sawyer had told him about finding Ben's day planner and other paperwork. It was obvious that more people were involved in what had taken place. He was also certain that whoever had been here was up to no good, and now they weren't here. But where was Ben? He could be laying out there in the dark, or he could be with whoever had been here. The only thing that seemed certain was that the other people who had been here would have some answers. The highest percentage chance of having any success and solving the riddle would be to track down and find the other people. There was mud and snow, which would make the tracking easier than if it had been dry. They would start tracking.

"No one went to the north across the creek, boss; they must have gone back south the same way we came in."

"Yeah, come on, we've got some catching up to do," Tommy replied.

They got back into Tommy's Dodge truck and started up and out of Birch Springs Canyon, and Tommy Davis became increasingly angry. Angry and worried. When they had crawled out of the canyon and reached the top of the ridge where there was cell phone coverage, he dialed Buster Saunders' number. Buster was the newly elected sheriff. Buster's phone rang until it went to voicemail. Hidalgo County, being a small and very poor county, had no one working at the sheriff's office at night. He left Buster a voicemail, "Buster, this is Tommy Davis. You need to call me as soon as you get this message."

Vidal Garcia Pizarro added another stick to his fire hidden in the rock pile where he had now been for over two days. Although his supply of drinking water from gallon jugs had been replenished twice by runners sent by the jefe, Ray Martinez, he was out of water again. He had supplemented his need for water by eating snow, but now the snow was almost totally gone and what little was left had freeze dried to the extent that its moisture content was minimal. He had just eaten his last can of Vienna sausages and all of the Jumex juice was gone. It was 10:30 p.m., and he had just watched the second set of headlights come and go in a three-hour period, in and back out of Birch Springs.

In the darkness of night, he could not distinguish for certain the description of either vehicle or its occupants, but his intuition and common sense told him that these last visitors were not friendly to the mission he was involved in. The timeframe had no doubt reached the point where someone would be searching for the poor gringo that the jefe and his cohorts had captured and were holding hostage. He felt sorry for the man, although he had never seen him. The gringo was collateral damage, an unfortunate byproduct of the Narco trade business.

Vidal had been in constant contact with Ray Martinez as well as the big bosses in Mexico just across the line at the cartel's ranch. He had reported all that he had seen for two days, including two U.S. Border Patrol vehicles that had come and gone earlier in the day. He had just talked to the jefe and informed him that the last set of headlights had not headed west through San Luis Pass but, instead, went east and seemed to be following the jefe's trail. The trail that was no doubt very visible in the mud and what little snow that was left. In this last conversation with the jefe, Vidal could tell that Ray was getting high, no doubt the result of taking speed (methamphetamine), or perhaps he was mixing a little speed with some weed he was smoking, or maybe he was licking a nasty mixture of cocaine and crude protein and rubbing it into his gums. The mules and scouts who worked in the smuggling trade called this chiva, and depending on the recipe, the high one got from chiva was instant and super effective.

For the last several days, Vidal had not witnessed the jefe's actions because of his duties at his lookout post, but, listening to him on the radio in the last few hours, he could tell the jefe was sounding euphoric and belligerent. Vidal knew that the unwanted side effects of what was probably a narcotic-induced high would be poor judgement. The mission would suffer and perhaps the gringo.

Vidal had, for all practical purposes, been abandoned. The jefe and the drugs had moved on without him, but he did not care, and so at 11:00 p.m. he shouldered his AK-47 along with what was left of his plunder and walked south. He had performed his duties and would be rewarded. Long before sunup he would be safe on the Mexican side of the line. He felt lucky because he had no desire to be going to Phoenix; and tomorrow when the federales flew their helicopters over Birch Springs, he would have vanished into the Sierra Madre.

Chapter Six
January 7, 2016
Evening

For obvious reasons, the jefe ordered some men to rearrange the dope load and make room somewhere for the bricks of dope that Ben had been made to ride on, causing his face to be pushed up into the ceiling of the truck's interior. No doubt the jefe realized that Ben would be of little use as a guide if he couldn't see straight ahead through the windshield.

The caravan fell off the rocky slope and descended into the canyon that flowed north toward the OK Bar and farther still to the Adobes cow camp, and eventually the XT cow camp that sat within walking distance of the paved Cloverdale Road. Ben rode in the front seat of the pickup with the jefe sitting against the passenger-side door and the man who seemed to be kinder than the others sitting behind the steering wheel.

As they descended down the slope into the headwaters of Adobe Creek, Ben looked off to the northwest and could see a few lights made very dim because of distance, but still slightly visible. *Perhaps*, he thought to himself, *they are a barn light at the XT or a light at some ranch house farther north toward Animas*. And then he saw the flashing lights of a vehicle racing south on the Cloverdale Road fifteen miles distance. The flashing lights gave him a rush of optimism. Surely they came from a sheriff's office vehicle or maybe a Border Patrol truck; someone connected with some law enforcement agency headed south in search of him. It gave him hope, and he reminded himself that the jefe himself had promised that when they came to a main road they would release him. The Cloverdale Road was certainly a main road: the main artery linking Animas to the vast emptiness of Las Animas Ranch.

"Mira a esos malditos tipos de la patrulla fronteriza! Creen gue nos atraparán. Decir ah! No nos atraparán!" The jefe's loud and unexpected exclamation broke the silence the men had experienced for several miles with nothing but the sound of the truck sneaking its way through the wilderness. "Pendejos tontos." the jefe added.

Ben understood enough Spanish to know the man was saying that whoever was driving those vehicles with flashing lights were stupid so and soes, and they weren't going to catch him. They were stupid fools or something worse. The jefe's expletives brought Ben out of his dream of freedom and being rescued by the sheriff or the Border Patrol. It brought him back to the reality of sitting next to a man who had not gotten a good night's sleep in three or four days but was now boosted up by some type of narcotic, and whose visage seemed to take on the eternal shape of an evil sneer. The jefe's eyes were open but seemed to Ben to be vacant, like a house that was about to be occupied by demons from outside. The man's head was stooped slightly forward as if tired but was simultaneously held erect by stimulants. Ben noticed that the jefe was drooling, with small droplets of dirty saliva dripping down his chin that had not been shaven for days. Ben could smell him. The jefe smelled like yesterday's refried beans and sweat.

Suddenly Ben was afraid again, afraid of this ogre who was obviously not in his right mind. Or at least that was how Ben now perceived the jefe. A man who was not operating in what one could call the realm of normality but, instead, was navigating through a hall of warped mirrors. Ben longed to reach the Cloverdale Road. The jefe had told him several times that they would let him go when they reached a major road. The Cloverdale Road was a major road.

The caravan descended into the canyon and reached the OK Bar where there was a well and old set of corrals, and they continued north; and the road now became more passable because Las Animas Ranch cowboys traveled this road coming from the north, and the Adobes Camp and the XT, both of which had married cowboys who lived and worked out of those camps. As they drove north with nothing but moonlight to guide them, Ben contemplated his options. He knew that the Border Patrol had its MSC ground radar unit set up near the XT Camp, and it was pointed south toward the Adobes and OK Bar, the very trail that the Narco caravan, which he was a part of, was traveling. He had seen the flashing lights many miles away, traveling on the Cloverdale Road and surmised that authorities had been notified that he was missing. He hoped that as the caravan went north it would eventually come into the ground radar unit's field of vision and range, and because of that the Border Patrol would have an ambush prepared and waiting somewhere up ahead; somewhere in the vicinity of the Adobes or the XT and the juncture of the dirt road they were on and where it reached the Cloverdale Road.

Ben thought that authorities from American law enforcement agencies could rescue him. He dreamed of being rescued. He hoped that friends were out looking for him. As these thoughts consumed him, he sat next to the jefe who occasionally came out of his self-absorbed fog and glanced at his topographical map in the dim light of his cell phone and asked Ben where exactly they were, but mostly, on this leg of the odyssey, they drove slowly and silently absorbed in their own thoughts. Sitting very close together, yet many miles apart.

The caravan drove by the old OK Bar corrals and windmill and proceeded down the canyon toward the Adobes Camp, and Ben became more apprehensive and yet excited. He was apprehensive about driving by the Adobes because the road passed very close to the ranch house, and the cowboy who lived there had a number of dogs, and the caravan would have to pass through a gate very close to the yard fence that surrounded the house. He could not believe they would be able to get by that place without setting off a volley of barking that would wake the dead. On one hand, he thought that would be a good thing because surely the man and wife would wake up and then look out and see the Narcos' dope-laden trucks and immediately call the Border Patrol or the sheriff. But he also feared that the lights coming on in the house and barking dogs might ignite some violent behavior out of his Mexican captors. He decided to try again to get them to turn him loose. "Why don't you let me go?" he asked the jefe.

"No, not yet. When we get to a main road, I will let you go."

They drove on, and when they reached the Adobes Camp they passed by the house and through the gate as if they were invisible. There wasn't a single peep out of a dog and no lights came on in the house nor was there any other sign of life at the camp, even though the gate they passed through was a mere forty yards from the back door.

They proceeded silently, running with no lights toward the XT seven miles farther. Even though Ben knew there was good cell phone service at the point in the road they had now reached, he, as well as the two men he was with, jumped when the Mexicans' phones began ringing. The jefe and driver had animated conversations with some people somewhere off in the distance. The two Mexicans were talking too fast for Ben to understand much of what was said.

Then the men reached a big set of corrals used to hold, sort, and ship cattle. There were several roads at this place that left the main road and disappeared, going in back of the corrals. The snow had been melted and gone at this place for at least a day, and there was evidence of other vehicle traffic. Suddenly the jefe ordered the caravan to turn off the road they were traveling and onto one of these side roads. They drove a ways, perhaps a half-mile, and stopped behind a hill with some trees and brush on it. At that point, for the first time, Ben was able to see that there were five pickups in the caravan. He was still not blindfolded because the jefe had not replaced it after asking for his guidance the last time they had left Birch Springs which was now about eight hours earlier. But his hands were still tied together.

The engines were turned off in every truck, and for a while they sat there silently, as if hiding. And then, as if on cue, the jefe opened the passenger side door of the truck and stepped out while motioning the driver to follow. Ben was told to stay put, sitting in the front seat. After several minutes, the driver, still being the one who was the kindest of his captors, returned and got Ben's lunchbox, which held Ben's cell phone, and left with the lunchbox and phone in his possession. Ben sat in the cab of the truck while the jefe and some, or maybe all, of the men from the other trucks held a conference somewhere out in the darkness of night. Finally the driver reappeared and told Ben, "When this is all over, this is where you will find your stuff." Then the man disappeared again, and Ben figured he was referring to his lunchbox and cell phone. The jefe and driver returned and joined Ben in the truck, and they all continued to sit as if still waiting for something.

Finally the jefe gave the signal to start their engines and pull out from their hiding place, and they got back on the main road that ran between the Adobes Camp, the XT, and the Cloverdale Road, which was now about a half mile away. A stocking cap was produced, and the jefe put it on Ben's head and pulled it all the way down to his chin, covering his ears and face; but this was a poor excuse for a blindfold because Ben could see enough through the small holes to have a pretty good idea where they were.

"Why don't you let me go?" Ben told the jefe. "You told me you would let me go when we got to a main road, and now we are here at a main road." Through the holes in the stocking cap, Ben could see that they were pulling out onto the pavement of the Cloverdale Road, and he realized that a pasture gate, which in his experience had always been kept closed, was now open; and the caravan drove through the open gate without having to slow down or stop.

The jefe answered his question, "No, we are going to keep you with us a little longer."

For hours Ben had ridden along in the truck in between the driver and the jefe, Ray Martinez, envisioning an ambush where the Border Patrol and sheriff would be hiding and waiting for the caravan to reach the Cloverdale Road. With its MSC scope truck parked near the spot where the Adobes Road left the Cloverdale Road, the scope truck should have been watching them for several hours. He had seen the scope truck parked in that very spot for weeks. It had been there the morning before as he drove south toward Birch Springs and the easy job of installing a new relay switch in the dozer. But now as the caravan drove past the very spot where the MSC unit had been parked twenty-four hours earlier, he could see through the holes in the stocking cap, which the jefe had pulled over his face, that the radar unit was gone.

"Aye chingado, son las cinco de la mañana." And then changing to English the jefe continued, "We need to get going. I'm tired of this place."

"Si, yo tambien," the driver answered.

So, Ben thought, *it's five o'clock; they should be looking for me.* And then he realized he wasn't sure who "they" were. Would the Border Patrol be looking for him? Or the sheriff? Tommy Davis? Perhaps nobody. He thought they would be waiting for them when they got to the Cloverdale Road, but they weren't. The jefe broke Ben's private train of thought by passing a long gust of wind, "Eso se sintio bien." The vulgar Mexican exclaimed as he chuckled out loud.

God help me, Ben thought, and they drove north toward Animas, five trucks loaded with dope, ten Mexicans, and a kidnapped gringo on a lost highway traveling with no headlights. Where was everyone at?

Chapter Seven
January 7, 2016
10:30 p.m.

Tommy Davis drove his 4-wheel drive crew-cab diesel truck faster than he would have if it had been broad daylight, even though it was late at night, bouncing and jarring the heavy truck along the boulder-strewn, primitive road. He was not a man who generally drove fast, as it was his belief that slowing everything down when operating in rough country saved time and money because a man created fewer breakdowns and stress on machinery. But he was now operating out of character, enough so that even his companion, Junior Garcia, noticed. He was determined to track down whoever had made the tire tracks in the snow and mud on these backroads east of Animas Peak. He hoped that whoever had made the tracks also had Ben Moody, and that Ben Moody was alive. The more Tommy thought about what he had seen, the more he was convinced that he and Junior were chasing drug runners. The evidence at Birch Springs—the pickup stuck in the mud, Ben's tools scattered all over, the tire tracks showing how someone had obviously tried to pull the truck out of the mud, and the small pieces of burlap they had found—all pointed to drug runners. Especially the pieces of burlap. He was convinced that Ben Moody had driven up on some outlaws, and they had either killed him and hidden his body somewhere, or they had taken him with them.

He drove on recklessly, at least compared to the way he usually drove, and followed the tire tracks made in the mud and snow. After he and Junior had traveled several miles he used his radio to call his wife. "Betty, listen, we found Ben's stuff layin' around all over the place at Birch Springs. There is a pickup stuck there in the creek with sign that someone tried to dig it out - unsuccessfully. I think it was Mexicans with a load of dope, and I think they took Ben's truck and left."

"What about Ben?" Betty interrupted.

"I don't know about Ben. We didn't find him. But I'm hoping they took him with them, but I don't know. He could be layin' out there in the brush, but I don't know. We decided to try and catch up to them, but there is tracks everywhere. Some tracks going south toward the Pass Road. Maybe they went back to Mexico or on toward the Culberson and Highway 81.

"Oh God, Tommy, . . . they could have killed . . ."

"I know. I know. Listen, we don't know anything at this point; we can't jump to conclusions. There's a lot of sign on a road going east toward Deer Creek, maybe they went that way. Someone for sure did, so me and Junior are following the sign and see if we can figure it out. I want you to call the Border Patrol and tell them what I'm doing. Tell them we got a man missing and maybe illegals have him. Tell them there's probably some dope involved. Tell them to look out for Ben's white Ford pickup."

"Shall I call Caroline? She has called me three or four times, and I told her I would call when I knew something."

"No, . . . no, I think for right now we better not say anything. Just call the Border Patrol. I tried to call the sheriff but got no answer. I left him a message. We are driving east toward Deer Creek. . . . Hell, they might be holed up at the Lynch. I don't know, but just try to get people looking for Ben's truck."

Tommy and Junior drove east on the ranch roads going toward Deer Creek, but it was slow going even though Tommy was punishing his new pickup much harder than he liked. Several times they encountered crossroads where vehicle tracks had gone several directions. Tommy knew the roads well enough to know that some of the roads that the people he was pursuing were on would end up at a dead end, but he followed every track anyway. He went and found where they had come to an impassable spot and turned around only to return and get back on the main road. He saw where at least one vehicle had become stuck in some mud but had been rescued by a second vehicle that had pulled it out. He evaluated the evidence left by the tracks and knew for certain that he and Junior were following more than one truck; he thought maybe as many as three or four, but he wasn't certain. He meticulously followed every possible lead hoping he could catch up to whoever it was he was chasing, hoping that somewhere up ahead he would find Ben Moody alive.

After following several false leads through the mud and rocks, Tommy and Junior finally reached the Deer Creek Road which led them on a course to the north by northwest. The tire tracks left by the trucks that Tommy believed belonged to Narcos seemed to wander about less than before, as if the men driving them had finally settled on a steady course that they were committed to follow, or so it seemed to Tommy. It was painfully slow going due to the lack of maintenance the road had received, but they trudged on with deliberation. When they reached the top of the divide where the landscape dropped in elevation out in front of them to the north, Tommy stopped his pickup for a minute and shut off his headlights. The two men sat silently staring out through the windshield. They could see the very faint glow of several lights many miles to the north. And then, suddenly, Tommy caught a glimmer of something reflecting off of the moon. It was just a flash, a passing glitter that was gone as fast as it had appeared on the ground somewhere in the distance, maybe three or four miles. It was moving. He was sure of it.

Junior had not noticed it, but Tommy Davis didn't care; he knew he had seen it, and in his mind he was sure it was light reflecting off of the window of a vehicle somewhere down below, maybe about the OK Bar, or close in that vicinity. He knew they were out there moving away from him, but he was determined that he would catch them.

Tommy pressed on the accelerator and fell off the hill bouncing and being tossed about in the rocks. He thought about turning his headlights off so he could be sneaky but knew that would be defeating his purpose which was to catch up to whoever was running out in front of him. If he was going to catch them he would have to use his headlights. *Let them run with no lights. He would outrun them with his lights on.*

As far as the OK Bar, the men he was pursuing were easy to track because they were the only people who had traveled that way in a vehicle for a long time, but when they reached the OK Bar, Tommy could tell the road had seen a lot more use in recent days because the cowboy who lived at the Adobes Camp had been in and out of there in a pickup. But the tracks, at least for now, had all stayed on the road and so they had no rabbit trails to confuse them.

When they reached the Adobes cow camp, the vehicle tracks went right through the gate and proceeded northwest toward the XT, but now, at several junctures of ranch roads, Tommy could see tire tracks going off to the right and left. Should he follow each piece of sign or should he stay on course? He felt like the freshest tracks were continuing on toward the XT, but he wasn't absolutely certain. His truck was now making dust because it had not stormed here as much as it had twenty miles to the south, and being lower in elevation meant the slight snowfall had melted much quicker and had been gone by ten in the morning the day before. Making his best guess as to what to do, Tommy chose to stay on the main road. He felt like he and Junior were about to overtake them, whoever "them" was. He decided to put all his cards on the table and bet that the people he was pursuing were just ahead.

Tommy could drive much faster now because they were off of the mountain and the country was sandier and the roads well-maintained. When they got to the XT shipping corrals he speeded up to as fast as forty miles an hour. As they rushed past the shipping corrals, Tommy was hoping they might catch up to someone by the time they reached the Cloverdale Road. In his mind he fully expected to see a major ambush taking place just ahead as he and Junior approached the XT Camp. He remembered the MSC radar unit parked close to where the Adobes Road left the Cloverdale Road and went to the southeast toward the Adobes and the OK Bar. He knew that Betty had phoned the Lordsburg Border Patrol Station and had given them all the information he had conveyed to her five or six hours earlier. He knew beyond the shadow of a doubt that he had seen the moon reflecting off of a vehicle that was north of his position when he was on the divide where the Adobe Creek drainage started and ran this direction. Moonlight on a vehicle that would have to reach the confluence of the Adobes Road and the Cloverdale Road. The vehicle would have to travel straight into the sites of the Border Patrol radar. He hoped that the outlaws were even now being tied up by federal agents who had ambushed them when they reached the Cloverdale Road.

Tommy Davis and Junior Garcia pulled up to the edge of the pavement on the Cloverdale Road at exactly ten minutes before five on the morning of January 8, and the silent emptiness that lay before them was eerie. There was nothing. Where his imagination had great events taking place, they saw nothing. The Border Patrol's MSC unit was gone. Only hours before, it had been there, but now it was gone.

There was nothing. Only blackness, and a moon and stars to witness a vast nothingness. Tommy got out of his pickup and stared down the Cloverdale Road, both to the north and then to the south. He saw nothing. Somewhere off in the distance, he heard a coyote howl and then howl again, but there was no ambush. He called his wife, "Betty, have you heard anything? Did you call the Border Patrol? What's going on?"

"Yes, Tommy, I have talked to the Border Patrol several times. I relayed your information. The last I heard they think Ben has been taken into Mexico."

"Betty," Tommy almost screamed into his cell phone, "I'm here at the XT and the Cloverdale Road, and nobody's here. The Mexicans came by here, I'm sure! Where's the MSC unit? Why wasn't someone here waiting for us? I think the outlaws came here and then went either north or south. Why wasn't someone waiting for us here?" Now Tommy was shouting. He hadn't slept all night, and Ben was still gone.

"I don't know, Thomas! I don't know. They just told me that they think the outlaws were trying to get back to Mexico."

"Mexico? Hell, I think I saw them ahead of me going north down about the OK Bar. Why would they think they were going south? Why wasn't someone waiting for us here at the XT?"

"I don't know, Thomas. I'm just reporting what they told me."

"Have you talked to Caroline?"

"Yes, several times. The kids are all there with her."

"Have you told her we think Ben's been kidnapped?"

"No, I haven't said anything. She thinks he's broke down somewhere."

"Good, don't tell her anything. Call the Border Patrol again. Call the sheriff." Tommy Davis sat deflated holding the cell phone to his ear and staring out onto the pavement of the Cloverdale Road. "I don't know what to do. I thought they would be waiting for us when we got to the pavement. But hell, there's nothin'. I don't know what to do. I guess we will go south toward the headquarters and the Fitzpatrick. I don't know what else to do."

Tommy Davis turned to the left, straight south toward Mexico. After a few miles they came to the Border Patrol forward operating base, and then a few miles farther south, they passed Las Animas Ranch headquarters and continued south toward the Fitzpatrick Flat and the Mexican border. When he reached the intersection where the road toward San Luis Pass turned left, toward the east, and the road toward Cloverdale, which was west, Tommy Davis and Junior Garcia drove up to a lone Border Patrol agent sitting quietly in the cab of his pickup staring into the blackness of early morning in the wintertime. The agent was performing a task known as sitting-on-the-X, which signifies positioning oneself at a predetermined place and responding however seems appropriate to any given scenario that might present itself.

Tommy Davis pulled up beside the Border Patrol agent just as the horizon was turning lighter in the eastern sky. "How are you this morning?" He asked the agent who had happily rolled down his window enough that they could be heard over the sound of diesel-truck engines, "Have you seen anything similar to Ben Moody's pickup?"

"I'm sorry, sir, but I don't know what you're talking about."

"We've got a man missing, and we think he's been kidnapped by Narcos over at Birch Springs yesterday. We trailed them around the east side of the mountain last night. We reported it to the Lordsburg Border Patrol Station last night. You don't know about it?"

For a moment they just stared at each other, and then the federal agent replied, "No, sir, I don't know what you are talking about."

Chapter Eight
January 8, 2016
5:00 a.m.

The Narco caravan pulled out onto the Cloverdale Road and turned to the right, which was north, and proceeded toward Animas fifteen miles away. At that point, Ben Moody was still riding in the lead pickup sitting in between the jefe, who was riding shotgun, and the kinder man, who was driving. All five trucks were traveling with no lights, and, because of that, they were going fairly slow, about twenty-five miles an hour, but they were in an orderly fashion, at least as much so as traveling with no lights could afford. Ben could see glimpses of the night through the knitted construction of the stocking cap that covered his face; mainly he would catch the glitter of stars in the night sky or the reflection of the moon across a window or the hood of the pickup. He was still handcuffed with plastic ratchet-strap type material, like one would find wrapped around some product in a hardware store. He had wiggled his hands enough that he was sure he could get loose if he needed to but thought it best to keep this development to himself.

Driving on the pavement of the Cloverdale Road seemed to bring new electricity to the Mexican crew. There was much activity on the Mexicans' phones, especially the jefe's, who was texting and having repeated and very animated conversations with someone or several different people. The talk that Ben heard was too fast for him to determine exactly what was being said. After going a mile or so to the north, one of the trucks pulled out and around the lead truck and then accelerated and went out of sight. After several minutes the jefe received a call from someone talking loudly, and the jefe then exploded into instructions telling the driver to turn left and go off the road. The pickup bounced and lurched forward, and Ben heard the scraping and stretching sound of a barbed-wire fence that they were crashing into and breaking, and they drove out through the rocks and brush and came to a stop in a cow pasture. They had turned around enough to be pointed back toward the Cloverdale Road. After several minutes, Ben saw, through the stocking cap, the lights of a vehicle going south. He imagined that it was someone looking for him, but he had no way of knowing if that was true.

After the vehicle passed, they continued on to the north, only now they stayed out in the cow pasture bouncing through rocks and brush and clumps of grass. Several more barbed-wire fences were breached with the stretching of wire and the sound of posts being pulled out of the ground. The fences did not slow the Mexicans down even a little bit, but, instead, they just kept driving.

Eventually, after several miles, they pulled out again onto the pavement of the Cloverdale Road, and this provoked new hope in Ben; and, in between the frequent conversations the jefe was having, Ben said, "When we get to Animas will you let me go?"

The jefe answered in a way similar to a grownup answering a small child who is pestering the adult about something, but the grownup really isn't paying much attention to the child. "Yes, we will let you go."

Soon they were drawing close to town, and Ben looked off to the left, and even though his house was a half mile off the road, he could tell that it was lit up like a Christmas tree. He knew Caroline was in there. Probably some of his kids had rushed home to be with her. Probably they were worried sick. He wondered if the sheriff, or the Border Patrol, or Tommy Davis, or someone had told her that he likely had been kidnapped by drug runners. He wondered if they thought he was dead. He wondered if Caroline was in tears. And then he realized that he was letting his imagination run wild. Caroline was a lot sturdier than to be crying, and then he thought that maybe she was mad as hell, and then he realized for the second time that his imagination was running wild; and it occurred to him that maybe he was feeling sorry for himself. He hadn't slept for twenty-four hours. His head was making a buzzing noise, and a slight tingling sensation had spread throughout his body; and between the strands of yarn in the stocking cap covering his face, he saw that they had reached the intersection of Highway 9 where the Cloverdale Road ended and evolved into northbound New Mexico Highway 338. He could see they were passing the livestock brand inspector's house on the right and the Baptist church on the left. They continued on north on 338 toward Cotton City, and the jefe lifted his left leg and a very loud fart exploded out into the cab of the pickup. "Ah chingao, que Bueno, no?" The jefe roared with laughter.

"God help me," Ben said under his breath and watched as the village of Animas disappeared behind them.

Caroline Moody had been up most of the night except for several attempts to lie down and get some sleep.

She had showered and mechanically accomplished her nightly toilet and had started to dress in sweatpants, but on second thought she had dressed in denim Wranglers and a shirt and looked as if she was ready to go outside and do the chores. Betty Davis had called her three or four times and given her updates about Tommy and Junior driving around Las Animas Ranch looking for Ben.

Caroline was under the assumption that Ben had gone off somewhere on the big ranch to the south, for some unknown reason, and was probably broke down in a remote place. She was all too aware that there were a thousand square miles of remote places south of her house. Nothing had been said about finding a truck with Mexican plates stuck in the mud at Birch Springs. Nothing was said about Ben's tools being scattered about near the stuck pickup. Nothing had been said about the possibility that Ben had been kidnapped by illegal aliens who were running drugs.

Caroline thought about calling her four children and asking them to come and be with her, but a dozen times she fought off the urge to do so. Finally, at ten o'clock, she gave in and called all of them one by one and explained that their father was missing. He had left in the morning saying that he would be home at midday, and they had planned on spending the rest of the day together, but he had not returned. Tommy Davis and some other people, although she wasn't sure who, were out looking for him, but so far they had been unsuccessful in their attempt to locate his whereabouts.

The four kids, two boys and two girls, all responded, yes, they were coming: two from Tucson, 100 miles away; one from Lordsburg, 42 miles away; and one from Deming.

The last child to arrive was the oldest daughter, Tamara, who lived in Deming and worked for the Luna

County Attorney's Office. She had worked late and did not arrive at Ben and Caroline's house until 1:30 a.m. the morning of January 8.

Earlier in the evening, Caroline had seen two vehicles pull off of the Cloverdale Road and park about halfway between the highway and the house. The vehicles had stopped and shut their lights off. When Tamara arrived and walked into the house, the first thing that Caroline asked her was, "What are those two cars parked out there?"

"One is a Border Patrol pickup and the other one is a dark-colored Suburban. It's solid colored like maybe some kind of law enforcement. They are just sitting there." Tamara said, and then continued, "Any news about Dad?"

"No, nothing."

The truck with Ben and the two Mexicans continued north on Highway 338 headed toward Cotton City, and then on the south edge of that small village, the pickup the three of them were riding in had a flat tire. The jefe ordered the driver to turn off of the road to the right, which was east, and they entered an alfalfa field.

They lurched and bounced along for several hundred yards and came to a stop. The jefe was busy talking to people on his cell phone, cursing and issuing oaths and blasphemies amid orders. For a few minutes they sat there, and then the sound of other vehicles coming to a stop somewhere nearby could be heard.

The jefe and driver got out of the truck and conversed with some other men who had come walking up from vehicles that had stopped somewhere close by. Suddenly someone grabbed a hold of Ben and pulled him from the cab of the truck where he still sat, and two men took his arms and began leading him through the alfalfa stubble. He tripped in the rut of a tire made by the large irrigation pivot that watered the alfalfa. The two men who were leading him cursed and lifted him to his feet. One man lifted the stocking cap that had blindfolded him from off his head and threw it down, cursing as he did so, and they walked on through the field. With his new freedom of sight, Ben could tell that neither one of the men were the jefe nor were they anyone he had seen close enough to recognize, but he was sure they were part of the bunch he had been with since Birch Springs.

They stood on the edge of the field for a few moments and then heard the sound of a vehicle coming, but it, too, had no lights. One of the two men walked off and disappeared. "Are you going to turn me loose now?" Ben asked.

"No," the man said curtly, "you are going to stay with us a while longer."

The man kept putting his hand in his jacket pocket as if he was checking on something. Ben surmised it was a pistol. "Are you going to shoot me?" Ben inquired.

"No, not unless I am told to." The man, pointing, gestured to the sound of the approaching vehicle, and they walked up to what turned out to be Ben's own pickup. Piled high on the bed was a very large load of something that had been covered by a big tarp and strapped down. Ben surmised that it was marijuana. Whoever had been driving the truck got out and walked away leaving Ben alone with just the one man who kept checking whatever was hidden in his coat pocket. The man ordered him to get in the truck while he himself got in behind the wheel, and when he got the truck fired up they took off to the north driving on Highway 338, but after a short distance they turned left on a dirt road and drove quite a ways and then turned out into a cow pasture. There was a considerable amount of mesquite, salt brush, and other types of vegetation which they drove through for a ways, and then they stopped and the Mexican got out and ordered Ben to do the same.

The man became very busy unstrapping the tarp which he threw on the ground when it was loose, and then he began unloading the large bales of dope while Ben stood watching. Suddenly the man turned on him and said, "Are you going to help me?" Ben maneuvered to the opposite side of the pickup bed and just stared at him. "You are going to help me!" the man demanded angrily.

Ben took his hands that were still tied and started dragging bales of dope toward the edge of the pickup but staying on the opposite side of the truck. It was beginning to get light in the east. The man looked at Ben and said, "What's the matter? You don't trust me?"

"Well, right now I don't trust anyone."

The Mexican stared at Ben for a moment and then shrugged his shoulders and both men went back to work. Ben drug bales toward the edge of the pickup bed, and the man stacked them in a nice pile on the ground. The Mexican now walked to the cab of the truck and, upon looking inside, he found several small bricks of dope that had been laid under the seat. This find sent the Mexican into a rage, and although he spoke English he cursed Ben profusely in Spanish, "Tonto! Tonto culo. Por que no puedes hacer nada bien?" Ben stared at him while the man continued cursing.

Finally, being satisfied with their work, the Mexican covered the large stack of marijuana with the tarp and then wrapped the straps around the bundle to hold the tarp securely in place. He ordered Ben to get in the truck, and they drove north a ways and presently came to a gate in a fence. The man stopped the truck. Ben started to get out and open the gate, but the man motioned him to sit still. The Mexican reached in his coat pocket, as if to remind Ben of his gun, and then got out and opened the gate. *This is interesting,* Ben thought. *This is the first time all night we've stopped at a gate. Every other time we just crashed through the fence.*

They hit a gravel road and turned right. It was light enough that Ben recognized they were traveling on McCarty Road. In the ever so pale early morning light, Ben could make out the turbine blades on a young pecan orchard. "You can let me go now. I'm no danger or trouble to you." Ben said.

"No," the Mexican answered. "You and I are good friends, and we are going to your house, and me and some of my friends are going to stay with you for a few days." The thought of this scenario sent a rush of fear through Ben, considering that having a bunch of Narcos hiding in his house might be more than he could live with.

They pulled up near the corner of McCarty Road and Highway338, and the man ordered Ben out of the truck. The two men met at the back of the truck with Ben not knowing what to expect. The Mexican took a knife and cut the plastic strap that had kept Ben handcuffed. "You are going to drive now," the Mexican announced.

They had stopped a hundred yards away from the pavement, and Ben approached Highway 338 thinking he would turn to the right, or south, which would lead back to Animas. He stopped and turned the steering wheel to the right, but the Mexican put his hands up to stop him. Off to the south, a mile or so away, they could see the flashing red lights of some kind of law enforcement vehicle stopped on the highway. The Mexican pointed to his left, or to the north. "No, no, no, we are going to Benson," he motioned Ben to drive on toward Interstate 10.

"Why are we going to Benson?" Ben asked.

"I have friends there, and we are going to stay with them for a few days."

Caroline Moody had slept very little and by 7:30 a.m. on January 8 she was feeling desperate. She had talked to Betty Davis a half hour earlier, and Betty had given her no news. Betty had relayed the fact that Tommy and Junior had been looking for Ben throughout the night but had been unsuccessful in their search. Caroline had been told that Ben's pickup was also missing, and they had tried tracking it but had not found it. She had been told that Tommy and Junior were still, even at that moment, out looking for Ben. Betty had advised Caroline to be calm, that surely there was some reasonable explanation, and Ben would turn up safe and sound. Tommy and Betty Davis were more than just employers, they were trusted friends; and Betty's words meant a lot to Caroline, but even then she was still stressed.

Caroline continuously looked out her kitchen window toward the Cloverdale Road longing to see Ben driving in; but every time she looked away disappointed. And now, every time she looked that direction she saw the white Tahoe with the green stripe and Border Patrol insignia on the door just sitting there in her driveway several hundred yards from her door, and next to it was a charcoal colored shiny Suburban with dark tinted windows parked ominously, as if it was waiting to pick someone up, or perhaps let someone out. She could see a lone Border Patrol agent sitting behind the wheel in the Border Patrol Chevy Tahoe, but the darkened windows hid the secret contents of the Suburban. She became angry and thought to herself, *Who the hell do they think they are?*

At a quarter to eight, Buster Saunders, the newly elected county sheriff, drove up and came walking to the door. He knocked. "Come in," Caroline said apprehensively. Was he a harbinger of bad news? Buster entered the kitchen looking glum. Caroline looked at him for a moment fearing what she might hear, but he said nothing. *So what,* Caroline thought, *he always looks glum.* "Sit down, Buster. You want a cup of coffee?"

"Yes, Caroline, thank you. I've been up since four, so I need some." They stared at each other, and she waited for him to elaborate, but he stared at her in silence. She turned and got a cup and poured him some coffee that was already made and was hot. She turned and sat it before him, and then she stepped back. He stared at her.

Tamara broke the silence that had enveloped the room. "Hello, Buster," Tamara said as she walked up and extended her hand. He rose out of his chair with his cowboy hat in his left hand, and taking her hand he shook it. "So where's my daddy?"

The question rang out like a fire alarm. Buster obviously swallowed the lump that was in his throat. He sipped some hot coffee. He didn't like his coffee scalding hot, but he needed time. "We don't know where Ben is, but we are about to find him, I'm sure!"

"About?" Tamara questioned rather sternly. "What the hell is that supposed to mean?"

Caroline was backed up and leaning against the kitchen counter and staring at Buster who tried another attempt at the coffee. Buster said, "I got a call this morning, and they thought Ben was seen down below the Pass Road, down around the Lang or maybe the McKinney Flat. They offered to let me go up with them and look around."

"Who is 'they'?" Tamara shot out. Tamara worked for the Luna County district attorney, and she had a lot of experience working around law enforcement personnel. Some of the experience was good and some of it wasn't. She wasn't intimidated by lawmen at any level.

"Well," the sheriff said, "the Border Patrol."

"The Border Patrol thought my dad was down close to the border? Doing what? Was he seen there?"

"Uh, . . . well, . . . no, he wasn't seen there exactly, but for some reason, I don't know why, they thought he was there. We went up in a helicopter, and we flew the whole thing. From Antelope Wells to Cloverdale, but we didn't see anything. They let me out, and I came right back up here to talk to you." He picked his hat up and turned it around and around in his hands, then he put it down and sipped some hot coffee.

"Why do they think he was down on the border? He went to Birch Springs," Caroline interjected.

"I don't know, Caroline."

"Where do you think he is?" Tamara asked.

"I don't know, Tamara. We're lookin'. We're lookin'."

"Who are those people out there in those cars?" Caroline asked.

"I don't know, Caroline."

"Has anyone been out toward Hachita or Playas?" Caroline asked.

"No, Caroline, I don't think so," the sheriff stared at his coffee cup and nothing was said for about a minute.

"So what's going on, Buster?" Tamara asked with fire in her eyes.

"I don't know, Tamara! If I knew I would tell you, but I don't know. There's a Chevy pickup stuck in some mud below Birch Springs. They've been watching it for a couple days."

"Who's been watching it?" Tamara demanded almost coming out of her chair when she spoke.

"The Border Patrol."

A cold chill went down Tamara's spine. She stared at Buster Saunders trying to read more out of his expressionless face. She turned toward her mother trying to read from her expression if she had realized the implications of what the sheriff had said. Caroline didn't seem alarmed, and so Tamara turned back toward the sheriff, looking him square in the face.

"I need to go. As soon as we find out something, I'll let you know. We are looking."

"So you don't think anyone's been toward Hachita or Playas, or maybe the Young or the Timberlake?" Caroline asked.

"No - not yet. I need to go now." And he walked out the door.

❖

The sun was up, and it was broad daylight as Ben drove north through Cotton City with his Mexican companion riding shotgun. Ben had now been up for twenty-seven or twenty-eight hours having had no sleep with the exception of occasional chances to nod off for a few seconds at a time. He was running on pure adrenalin with a surreal consciousness maintained by stress. His truck was the only Ford pickup in Hidalgo County with a black flatbed having black toolboxes, and he hoped that the truck's uniqueness, coupled with the fact that by now everyone would know he was missing, would make someone notice he and the outlaw Mexican driving down the road.

Soon after passing the Valley View Church, about thirteen miles north of Animas, two Border Patrol vehicles came racing toward them with their red lights flashing. Ben thought about blinking his lights at them but remembered that all of the lights on his truck, both in the front and behind, had been knocked out and made useless. He then considered swerving into the oncoming lane a little bit, just to bring notice to himself. He even considered running head on into the lead Border Patrol vehicle. He knew without looking that the Mexican had his hand on his pistol and was ready to start shooting. The Border Patrol vehicles, one a Dodge pickup and the other a Chevy Tahoe, flew past driving at least eighty miles per hour.

"When we turn you loose we will know everything you tell the police," the Mexican said in a threatening tone of voice.

Ben gritted his teeth and said to himself, *Yeah! You assholes have knocked all of the lights out of my truck. You have thrown all my tools away. You have held me captive for a couple days. I think it is going to be pretty obvious what you've done to me!* He looked at the Mexican who stared back at him with what Ben thought was an overly confident expression.

They drove a little farther, and Ben noticed the fuel gauge on the dashboard. It showed that they had a quarter tank at the most. Ben knew the truck and all of its personal idiosyncrasies and was sure that in seventy or eighty miles they would run out of gas. He thought about mentioning that information to his companion but decided against it.

The Mexican continued to receive calls and what Ben thought were instructions, but he was unable to understand much. Soon after passing the two Border Patrol vehicles, Ben asked, "Can I please call my wife?"

The outlaw looked at him nonchalantly and replied, "No." End of conversation.

Right before they reached Interstate 10, a Hidalgo County sheriff's office patrol car exited the freeway, coming from the direction of Lordsburg, the county seat, which was now about eleven miles to the east. The sheriff's vehicle came toward them accelerating and racing south on Highway 338, and like the Border Patrol vehicles five minutes earlier, it went on by with lights flashing but never slowed down. When the deputy had passed, the Mexican grinned at Ben who drove onto the freeway and headed west toward Willcox, Arizona sixty miles away. Ben looked down at the fuel gauge.

For a long time they drove in silence, all the while Ben hoping that someone would recognize his truck and pursue them. He thought and imagined different scenarios about how that would play out. If, in fact, some kind of law enforcement officer did come screaming up behind them with sirens blaring—would the Mexican demand that he step on the gas and drive faster? That thought almost amused him. What little gas they had wouldn't last long with his foot pressing down hard. Perhaps the outlaw would tell him to stop fast, and he would leap out and start running out across the desert. Perhaps the Mexican would lean out the window and start shooting backward at the cop car.

About the time the two men drove past Bowie, the Mexican's phone went off, and when he answered it, he had a short but very loud conversation with someone. Then he hung up and handed Ben the cell phone and said,

"Call your wife." He forced the phone into Ben's right hand. Driving with his left hand, Ben dialed Caroline's cell phone number, all the while thinking, *What the hell is this about?*

When the phone started ringing on the other end, the Mexican heard it and said very plainly, "Tell your wife to go home!" *That's an odd statement*, Ben thought.

"Hello," Caroline answered.

"Where are you at?"

"Where are you at? What's going on? I've worried -

"Never mind. I'm alright. Where are you?"

"I'm out here at the Chalk Hill looking for you. The sheriff said no one had come out this way so I was going toward Hachita or the Timberlake."

The Mexican gave Ben a menacing look.

"Caroline, listen to me. I'm alright. I can't talk right now, but I'm alright. But it's very important that you go back home. Now!"

The Mexican motioned for him to hang up. They drove on for a moment, and the man's phone went off again. He accepted the call and then handed it to Ben.

"Where are you? What has happened to you?" It was Caroline.

"I'm almost to Willcox. I'm alright, but I can't talk right now. You need to go home and stay there." The outlaw grabbed the phone out of Ben's hand and stopped the call.

Ben drove past the exit where Highway 191 turned north toward Safford and looked at the outlaw, "We are almost out of gas."

"How far?" the man asked.

"We might make it to Willcox."

The Mexican contemplated this for a moment and asked, "You got any money?"

"No, you guys left my wallet down at the shipping corrals south of Animas."

The outlaw thought about that information for a moment, and Ben asked, "You got any money?"

"No."

Ben almost laughed out loud. Suddenly he wasn't afraid of this guy or his gun or this whole dog-and-pony show he had been forced to be a part of.

The outlaw dialed a number on his cell phone, and a considerable amount of profanity and loud talk filled the interior of the truck. The man started giving Ben instructions, but the Mexican's ability to explain what he wanted in English broke down, and Ben couldn't understand what he was saying. Finally the man handed Ben the phone, and someone on the other end successfully communicated instructions for Ben to pull into the TA truck stop on the north side of the middle exit at Willcox and let the Mexican out. But Ben was also told that when he got home he was supposed to tell the authorities that he was turned loose on a remote dirt road out in the country. The man talking to him on the phone emphasized that the police should not be told that he let his Mexican companion out at the truck stop.

With renewed hope Ben pulled off the freeway and drove into the parking lot at the TA truck stop, and as if they were in mutual agreement that they hated each other, Ben's passenger opened the door and bolted, barely pausing to get the door slammed shut. Ben had not come to a complete stop, and when the outlaw's door closed, he pushed on the accelerator and spun his rear tires trying to make sure their separation was permanent. Several people who were standing nearby fueling their cars up started jumping up and down and hollering at Ben, for some reason, but he was not going to stop for anything or anybody. His mind raced, wondering what in the world the people might be hollering at him about. Were they trying to warn him that some outlaws were pointing guns at him. Maybe they noticed that his lights had all been knocked out. It didn't matter, he wasn't sticking around.

In his predicament, having no money, the only thing Ben could think of doing was to drive to an office where his sister-in-law worked and ask her to loan him some money for gas and to borrow her cell phone to call Caroline and tell her he was alive and would be coming home.

When he pulled up and parked in front of the business office and got out he immediately noticed a tree branch sticking out from under his truck. He bent down and saw that a large limb off of a mesquite tree was snagged quite securely to the truck's chassis, and they had been dragging it underneath, no doubt, since they had unloaded the dope out in the desert on the southwest side of Cotton City. Crashing through the cow pasture, the limb had been run over and became connected to the truck. The people hollering at him at the truck stop had no doubt noticed it, but the deputy sheriff and the two Border Patrol agents north of Cotton City had not.

Chapter Nine
January 8, 2016
Midday

Ben walked into the office where Caroline's sister worked and asked the receptionist if he could speak to his sister-in-law, and the receptionist told him that she had taken the day off. *Man*, Ben thought, *I'm not having very good luck!*

"Well, could you let me use the telephone? I need to call her."

The lady behind the counter stared at him. He was very dirty. He hadn't shaved in a couple of days. He didn't smell very good. "No," the lady replied.

"Ma'am, I'm kinda in a bind. I'm broke, and I'm out of gas in my truck, and I need to get back to Animas." He was now pleading. He started to tell her he had been kidnapped but then thought he should keep that to himself. The lady held her head at an angle like someone who is studying some curiosity such as pollywogs in a mason jar. She handed him a cordless telephone, and he phoned his sister-in-law and explained in a little more detail what his predicament was. The lady behind the counter cocked her head even further off center. Her eyes widened, and when the sister-in-law gave him instructions on where to meet her, Ben handed the phone back to the lady and walked out leaving her staring at his back.

Caroline's sister gave him enough money to fill his truck up with gas and buy a hamburger, and when those things were accomplished, he left Willcox driving east on Interstate 10. He began processing all of the events of the last twenty-six hours. After thinking about it while driving twenty-five miles, he decided that he better turn south on Highway 80 and go to where 80 and Highway 9 come together six miles north of Rodeo and then go east through Animas on that route rather than returning on Highway 338, the way he had traveled with the outlaw. He surmised that perhaps the Narcos would be hiding somewhere on 338, and letting them see him might not be a good idea. Again he felt the need to phone Caroline so he pulled into a gas station at San Simon and walked into the office and asked the girl behind the cash register if he could use her cell phone. Like the lady behind the counter at Willcox, the girl looked him up and down wondering what his story was but finally relented and handed him her phone.

"Caroline, this is Ben. I'm in San Simon on my way home, and I wanted to tell you that I'm going to drive down Highway 80 instead of coming through Cotton City. I don't want to run into any of my outlaw friends on the way home." At this the girl behind the cash register really looked at him. Caroline tried to question him and get more information, but he just said, "No, no, I'm alright, but I'm turning south at Road Forks and coming home that way. I'll see you at the house." He handed the girl her phone and walked outside and got in his truck and drove away, and, in doing so, left another woman staring at his backside with a puzzled expression on her face.

He drove east on Interstate 10 until he reached the junction known as Road Forks where he turned south on Highway 80 and followed that route for twenty-five miles and then turned onto Highway 9 and proceeded fourteen miles to Animas. When he reached Animas and drove by the Valley Mercantile he saw several state police cars parked there, as well as several Border Patrol vehicles. He drove on to the junction where Highway 338, Highway 9 and the Cloverdale Road met and saw more law enforcement vehicles. He went south, and when he turned off of the Cloverdale Road to go to his house, there were several more Border Patrol vehicles parked, as well as a charcoal-colored Suburban with tinted windows. Ben could feel all of the federal agents staring at him as he passed. Several federal vehicles were parked close enough to his house that the agents and officers sitting in their cars could stare at him as he walked into his home.

When he got into the house with no one there except him and his family, they had a reunion for sure. There was a little crying, happy crying, the type that comes with relief, and hugs and laughter and questions: What happened? Who was it? Did they hurt you? Were you threatened? Are you alright? He sat down, mentally drained. He was happy and relieved, but exhausted. Caroline and the children could sense his need to rest, and they backed off with the questions and talk and let him come down off of the high that he had maintained with a mixture of stress, anger, and fear. He tried to relax and then they came knocking. Two officers from the New Mexico State Police. Could they please ask him a few questions?

For a few moments Ben stared at them blankly. *Surely this could wait until tomorrow,* he thought. Everyone in the room stared at him.

"We would like to go to the community center; we have set up a command center there," one of the officers said. "We don't want to invade the privacy of your home."

Ben thought the officers were on his side. They were just doing their job, but he was tired. He had not slept more than five minutes in over thirty-two hours. He had just been drug through a knothole by dangerous people, but, yes, he would talk to them. "Okay," he said.

His daughter, Tamara, the strong one, got up and went outside with him; and they walked to her car. She had a degree in criminology and had worked with law enforcement and in the judicial system. She wasn't afraid of anybody. She and Ben got in her car and started following the two officers from the state police who were leading them back to Animas. "You don't have to talk to them, Dad."

Ben sat in the passenger side of the car. *I'm too damned tired to think,* were the words that came into his head, but he answered Tamara, "I'm not sure what to do."

They pulled up to the Animas Community Center and saw several state police cars parked, plus several Border Patrol vehicles and some other unmarked cars. When Ben got out of the car, Tommy Davis came walking toward him and shook his hand. Ben knew without a shadow of a doubt that he could trust Tommy. "I guess they are wanting to ask me some questions," he told Tommy.

"Yeah, they are going to hound you for information. I think it's a good idea to talk to them a little. Answer a few questions and then we will get you home. It won't take long."

A short and rather portly man who was in his late sixties was standing to one side near the door, and he approached Ben. He was Shorty Carraway, the pastor of the Animas Baptist Church. Shorty had made his living as a truck driver and mechanic before entering the ministry, and he still worked as a mechanic repairing heavy equipment for Tommy Davis. Shorty was not one who forced his opinions on people and would think about what he was saying before he said it. People around Animas respected him even if they didn't attend his church. Ben did not attend Shorty's church regularly, but he and Shorty were good friends. Shorty walked up to Ben and offered to shake hands, and then speaking quietly he told Ben, "You don't have to talk to these people if you don't want to." The two men looked at each other for a moment, and Ben shrugged his shoulders as if to say he didn't care. Actually, he was now so tired he couldn't think straight.

They walked inside the building. Ben recognized Sheila Garcia, a lady he had known for years and who was a trusted friend. She was an officer with the state police and was in full uniform. She smiled warmly at Ben. Ben was offered a chair next to a table and he sat down. The officers all introduced themselves. Ben immediately forgot all of their names, except Sheila's; but he noticed several of the state cops had called themselves investigators. One of the Border Patrol agents had introduced himself as the patrol agent in charge at the Lordsburg station.

Animas, New Mexico was a spot on the map with a highway (Highway 9) running through it, going east and west, and Highway 338 leaving and going north, and on paper the town looked as if it had some importance; but the truth was it didn't amount to much. Its main attractions were the public school with about 300 students in all twelve grades, a very fine ranch supply store known as the Valley Mercantile, and a tire shop with an employee or two. It also had a café that was closed most of the time and a Baptist church, regularly attended by a dozen people. A couple dozen homes clustered around these establishments in a scattered fashion. There was no town square or courthouse, and the several streets that lay off of the highway were bare dirt that was muddy when it rained, which was seldom, and dusty the rest of the time. But when word got around that Ben Moody had been found, the rumor mill burst into action as if it was Times Square. Outlaw Mexicans had abused him, according to some, while others hinted that because he had returned home under his own power, it surely meant he was in a partnership with the outlaws; but, when questioned, no one would own up to starting the rumor that Ben was dirty.

Betty Davis was a fireball, and she let it be known to anyone she came in contact with that Ben Moody was no drug runner or friend to anyone trafficking narcotics from Mexico, or anywhere else for that matter. She was mad as hell, and she and her husband, Tommy, were going to stand by Ben Moody regardless of what anyone else's opinion might be.

Betty drove into the Moody place shortly after Ben and Tamara drove away to attend the interrogation that law enforcement people were wanting to have with Ben. She had someone with her who got in Ben's pickup, the truck the Mexicans had borrowed to transport their drugs, and they delivered the pickup to a place in Animas which the state police had requested. The police wanted to inspect the truck and search for any and all evidence that they could find. Authorities had informed Tommy and Betty that they were going to go over the pickup with a microscope and fine-tooth comb. The Davis' were informed of this because they actually owned the vehicle and furnished it to Ben to use as his work truck.

The official inspection of the Ford pickup was a farce. The authorities released the pickup back into Tommy and

Betty's hands after a quick look over, and several days later when Tommy started cleaning it up and repairing damage (mainly electrical wiring and the damage to the lights) that had been done to it on the trip while loaded with drugs, Tommy himself found several small packets of dope stuffed into tool boxes that no one had yet found. The official government search had amounted to nothing.

❖

Forty miles west of Animas in Cochise County, Arizona, a cowboy and friend of Ben Moody's by the name of Jim Yarbrough heard about Ben's kidnapping early in the morning of January 8. Jim, a mercurial man with a short fuse and willingness to fight, was spurred into action when he received word through the supercharged rumor mill, that Ben had been set free by his outlaw captors in Willcox, which was a hundred miles north of Jim's cattle ranch. He was told that Ben had been deserted by his captors and left on the side of a dirt road outside of town. The rumors also said that Ben had been threatened and thoroughly terrorized.

Jim Yarbrough lived on a large cattle ranch on the Arizona side of the line, but earlier in his life he had worked on Las Animas Ranch and had ridden over much of the land in both counties. Jim had also been molested by outlaw aliens. His home had been burglarized multiple times, he had witnessed drive-throughs on his ranch, seeing pickup loads of dope coming across ranchland traveling off of the roads and laden with huge loads of marijuana; and upon reaching Highway 80 a few miles south of Rodeo, New Mexico, the trucks had proceeded north to places unknown, unhampered by the officials of any agency. One of his neighbors had been murdered by a Narco scout. He felt like he had seen it all, and now, a friend, Ben Moody, had been kidnapped and taken across state lines; and he knew enough about the law to know that because of that important detail Ben's case was now a federal offense. Jim was mad. The thought that Ben Moody, whom he had known for most of twenty years, was in some kind of partnership with a drug cartel never crossed his mind.

Jim did not trust the Border Patrol, but he knew the Cochise County sheriff and was friends with several deputies. He had a working relationship with them. One of those Cochise County deputies was Mark Ferrell, a ranch-raised kid now stationed in Willcox, and Jim knew that Mark Ferrell was a go-getter. He phoned Deputy Ferrell up, reaching him on his cell phone. "Howdy, Mark, this is Jim Yarbrough. Did you know about the cowboy from Animas who was kidnapped south of town by Narcos and taken with a load of dope and then turned loose in Willcox?"

"When did this happen?" Mark asked.

"Today, like a couple hours ago."

"Really? Where is he now?"

"He's back in Animas. I heard that the Border Patrol has him, and they are questioning him. I suppose the sheriff is there, but I don't know, but I heard they are asking him what happened. They've got him at the community center. I wondered if you thought you might be able to hunt down the kidnappers? Maybe they are still around Willcox."

"Wow, and this just happened today? Have you got some kind of description?" Mark asked.

"I don't, but I know some people over there, and if you're willing to look for the outlaws I can make a call and see if I can get some information. You interested?" Jim asked.

"Absolutely! I'm right here in town now, and I could get on it immediately, but I have to have some kind of description. I need information."

Prior to Buster Saunders becoming sheriff, Cochise County, Arizona and Hidalgo County, New Mexico had an agreement that they would allow and honor each other's help across both state and county lines. The area around the towns of Rodeo, New Mexico and Portal, Arizona, which were only six miles apart, was very remote, and neither county's law enforcement agency had enough resources to keep a deputy in the area full time. At any given time in either county, a deputy might not be any closer than fifty miles, so the two county sheriffs had agreed to welcome help coming from either direction in the case of an emergency. But, for some reason, when Buster Saunders was elected, this agreement was discontinued. Both Deputy Mark Ferrell and Arizona rancher Jim Yarbrough were aware of this development, but, perhaps, someone present at the Animas Community Center could get some pertinent information to Jim Yarbrough who could then relay it to Deputy Ferrell. They agreed that it was worth a try.

Jim Yarbrough knew Junior Garcia's cell phone number. Junior had been with Tommy Davis all night long trying to catch up to Ben Moody and his kidnappers. Junior was standing outside the Animas Community Center while Ben Moody was inside being questioned by the authorities. His cell phone rang and he answered it.

"Junior, this is Jim Yarbrough. Do you know where Ben is? Is he alright?"

"Yeah, he's alright. He's inside the building here. They're talking to him right now."

"Listen, I have a deputy friend in Willcox, and I told him what happened to Ben. I told him I thought the outlaws turned him loose near Willcox. He said he could start looking for them right now if he had some information. A description of the people, the car they were driving, where they were at, stuff like that. He wants to get on it right now. Do you know anything?"

"No man, I don't know nothin'." Junior peered into the doorway and could see Ben sitting in a chair with several people in uniform talking to him. "Looks like they got Ben, and they are talkin' to him right now."

"Is the sheriff there?" Jim asked.

"No, I haven't seen the sheriff."

"But is there a bunch of other officials there?"

"Yeah, there is a couple state policeman and several Border Patrol agents and a couple plain clothes guys. I don't know who they are."

"Listen, Junior," Jim said, "see if you can go in there and talk to one of those lawmen. Tell him you have a friend who knows a Cochise County deputy who's in Willcox right now, and if he had a description of the kidnappers and maybe a description of their car, he could start looking for them right now."

"Okay, I'll see what I can do," Junior said. Timidly he stepped into the community center, which was a large metal building with a cement floor, and he walked up to a Border Patrol agent standing on the outside perimeter of the officials gathered around Ben. Junior tapped the federal agent on the shoulder and, using his head, nodded to him hinting that he needed to speak to him. The agent followed Junior toward the door where Junior stopped. "Listen I've got a friend that knows a deputy sheriff in Willcox who wants to start looking for the outlaws but he needs a description. Any kind of information would help."

The Border Patrol agent looked at Junior suspiciously for a moment saying nothing, but finally replied, "Wait here, I'll go talk to somebody." He walked back into the building and approached a man in plain clothes and whispered in his ear. The man in plain clothes turned his eyes toward Junior who stood in the open doorway. The man then whispered back into the Border Patrol agent's ear and then the agent walked back to Junior and motioned him to step further outside. "They said, no. They don't want anyone's help! They are going to handle this by themselves." With that the Border Patrol agent walked back inside and left Junior standing alone in the cold sunshine.

❖

Ben sat in a metal folding chair next to a table in the community center. His daughter, Tamara was seated next to him as well as his son Rocky, who had shown up a little later. Ben looked at Sheila Garcia who smiled at him in a friendly way but said nothing. It was obvious that she wasn't running this show.

One of the Border Patrol agents who was in full uniform pulled up a chair and sat close to Ben and introduced himself. "Ben, my name is Claire Ainsley, I am the patrol agent in charge at the Lordsburg station. We just want to ask you a few questions."

"Okay," Ben said. "What do you want to know?"

"Well, you have been missing for a few hours, since yesterday morning actually. People were worried about you. They were out searching for you. Could you tell us where you have been?"

"I went down to Birch Springs to work on a dozer. I think I got there about mid morning yesterday."

"You think you got there? I mean, you got there, right? When did you get there?" the patrol agent in charge said.

"Well, I got there about in the middle of the morning yesterday."

"Okay, so you got there mid morning, say about ten. Tell us what happened then."

"I drove down to the well and turned down the draw, and that's when I saw the pickup. It was down the creek a ways, and it looked like it was stuck or maybe broke down. It was full of something in back, and there were some dope bales, or I thought they were dope bales, laying on the ground near the truck. I got spooked, and I turned around and tried to get outa there."

"You tried to get out of there? What do you mean, you tried to get out of there?" Claire Ainsley, the Border Patrol agent, was pressing him to answer.

"I mean, I turned around and started to drive out of the canyon. Drive out the same way I came in."

"Did you make it?"

"Yes, well, no; I mean I started out on the road. It is narrow and a good climb for a ways, and when I was going out I was stopped by a truckload of Mexicans, and they wouldn't let me go any farther."

"How do you know they were Mexican? Did you see their faces?"

"No, they had on masks, so the - "

"If you couldn't see them, if they had masks on, how do you know they were Mexican?" the agent asked.

"Well, I could tell they were Mexicans. They talked like Mexicans," Ben said.

"Then you speak Spanish?"

"No, not much -"

"How did you know they were Mexicans? You said that you don't speak Spanish. How did you know they were Mexican? Did they speak Spanish?"

"No, they spoke English. Well, mostly. They spoke Mexican and English, and I've been around a lot of Mexicans, and I know they were Mexicans." Ben had begun to speak at a faster pace. His heart was pounding and he felt tense.

"Were they from Mexico? Or Hispanic people from this side of the border. How can you be sure they were illegal aliens? Did you ask them? Did they tell you?"

"Of course I didn't ask them! I just know they were aliens. I've been around a lot of illegal aliens!" Ben had risen up out of his chair. He was now obviously shook up. His heart was racing and he told himself to relax. Taking a deep breath, he tried to calm down.

The patrol agent in charge seemed happy with the results of their conversation, and his voice became more condescending. "Tell us what happened next, Ben."

"They rushed my pickup and demanded that I get out and give it to them. They said they needed it. I told them to leave me alone, and I would leave and not say anything to anyone about what I had seen. They told me, no, that would be too dangerous."

"What would be too dangerous?" the patrol agent in charge asked

"I don't know what he meant. Why don't you tell me?" Ben replied.

Avoiding an answer to Ben's question, the patrol agent in charge said, "What happened next?"

"They pulled me out of my truck and tied my hands together and blindfolded me, and then threw me into the back of my truck, and we drove back down to the well."

"If you were blindfolded how did you know you went back to the well?"

"Because I know!" The question irritated Ben. He was about done and was very tired and stressed.

"Later on I saw glimpses of things, and I knew we were back down at Birch Springs."

"Did you fight back when they grabbed you?"

"Yes, but there was five of them and one of me."

"Tell us what happened next."

"I'm tired. I don't know how much more I want to say right now. The Mexicans threatened me and my family. They said they would know everything that I told law enforcement. I don't want to put my family in danger."

The patrol agent in charge feigned a slight chuckle as if he had been rehearsing the moment, and he said, "You are in no danger. People always say things like that. It's very common."

The patrol agent in charge continued talking and said, "So where did you end up?"

"In Willcox." Ben replied.

"They turned you loose in Willcox?"

"Yes," Ben answered.

Another agent spoke up for the first time during the interview, "Bullying tactics are always used in situations like yours, but I promise you - you are in no danger!"

"That's easy for you to say, but I was the one they were talking to, not you. I'm tired and I don't want to talk anymore," Ben said.

In a well-rehearsed, fatherly tone of voice, the patrol agent in charge said, "Yes, I can tell you are suffering from PTSD (Post Traumatic Stress Disorder). I also suffered from PTSD after my tour in Afghanistan. I know what you are going through. But trust me, you will be just fine in a few days."

Ben looked at the Border Patrol agent and thought to himself, *How do you know if I've got PTSD? Maybe the fact that I haven't slept for who knows how long might be part of my problem. Maybe part of my problem is that I'm sick of you!*

Ben thought these things but kept them to himself. He stood up, not realizing that he was acting very defiant. "I'm going home," he said and he walked toward the door with his two children.

"We would like to talk to you some more in a day or so," the patrol agent in charge said.

Ben turned and looked at him but did not have the strength left inside to answer. With no flicker of acknowledgment of the agent, he walked to Tamara's car, got in, and let her drive him home.

Chapter Ten
January 8, 2016
Late Afternoon

As Tamara and Ben drove home they passed three Border Patrol vehicles and a New Mexico state patrol car parked at the crossroads of the Cloverdale Road, Highway 338 and Highway 9, all in the vacant lot next to the brand inspector's house and across from the Baptist church. This was in addition to the law enforcement vehicles they had left behind at the community center, and when they got to the turnoff to Ben and Caroline's place there were two more Border Patrol Suburbans sitting there, and the charcoal-colored Suburban with tinted windows had also reemerged. Ben was now beginning to feel like they were not there to protect him but, instead, were watching him. "Damn!" he said out loud, "I wish they would all go away."

"You and mom need to pack up some things and come to Deming with me. They don't know where I live so you can get away from this for a few days. Get some rest and let this settle down."

Ben listened to what his daughter was saying, and he looked at the mysterious charcoal Suburban as they drove past it close enough to almost touch it. The windows were so dark you couldn't tell what was hidden inside. "Who in the heck is that?" Ben asked.

"Probably some federal agent wearing a suit and a

concealed weapon. You want me to go back and run him off?" Tamara asked.

"No, I think we need to take your advice and get out of here for a day or so."

They, along with Rocky who had followed them home from the community center, walked into the house and told Caroline of their plan to pack some things and leave for four or five days, try to recuperate, and come down off of the stress-induced high that they were experiencing. Caroline was all about it, and within minutes she was packed and ready to hit the road.

As Ben waited for Caroline to pack he commented to her about the spooky-looking Suburban, and she answered that it had been there most of the time since sometime in the middle of the night. To Caroline the charcoal Suburban had come to represent everything that was evil and unexplained about the last twenty-four hours. Going to Deming and leaving the Suburban behind was fine with her. She wanted to be alone with Ben; she was married to him, but even though he was back at home, she knew less about what had happened to him than just about everyone in town, or at least that is how she felt.

Ben and Caroline got in the back seat of Tamara's four-door truck, and with Rocky following in his own pickup, they all left Animas; all of them looking back over their shoulders to see if the charcoal Suburban, or maybe the jefe, was following them. They saw nothing and were thankful and began to relax. As they drove along, Ben was able, for the first time, to tell his story with some detail to Caroline and Tamara. They began the long journey of trying to put all of the pieces together and figure out what had happened. What they didn't know, and had no way of knowing, was the story hadn't ended yet, some of it had yet to be written.

Chapter Eleven
January 9, 2016
Early Morning

Early in the morning, about 7:30 on January 9, the day after Ben had returned home safe after his ordeal with the jefe and his compadres, Tamara Moody's telephone began ringing. She answered, and it was an officer with the New Mexico State Police office in Deming: an office of which she was familiar because of her work with the district attorney's office. They were hoping, the officer informed her, that she would bring her parents, Ben and Caroline, down to their office so they could ask Ben a few questions. They assured her that it wouldn't take long. They told her that it would be a big help to them and their investigation into the disappearance of her father and the subsequent ordeal that he had suffered through. It was very important, the officer said. Tamara told the man she would ask her father, and she would then call him back.

Ben and Caroline had been sitting at the kitchen table in Tamara's house drinking coffee. They would have gladly slept in, even all day for that matter, if they had been able to; but from years of experience getting up early and drinking coffee, they hadn't slept past five thirty. Old habits are hard to break. Tamara put down the phone and looked at her dad, "They want you to come down to the state police office and answer some questions." Ben looked back at her and considered this development. "You don't have to if you don't want to," Tamara said.

Ben had thought that they all would hide from everybody for a few days and try to relax. He hadn't had any nightmares in the night, but he had not slept all that well either, and when he was awake the memory of his twenty-six hours of captivity consumed his thoughts. He could not forget the menacing and threatening tone of the Mexicans' voices when they had told him, "We will know everything you tell the police." In his head he kept going over and over how he had been threatened. What exactly had they said? He would try to remember. He remembered how bold they had been when they had told him they were going to stay with him for a few days. They knew where he lived. He replayed the scene again and again when the man had told him to call his wife and tell her to go home. How had the Mexicans known exactly when Caroline left their house to look for him? Who was calling the Narco smugglers and telling them of Caroline's movements? Who was in the mysterious charcoal-colored Suburban? Why had the Border Patrol moved their radar unit away from the XT, a location from which surely they would have spotted him and the Mexicans as they approached the Cloverdale Road coming from the Adobes and OK Bar? Why had the sheriff been called south to the border to fly in a Department of Homeland Security helicopter when, in fact, the Border Patrol had been informed that Tommy Davis and Junior Garcia were tracking the outlaws north of Birch Springs and headed north toward Animas? Why had he and the Mexican left a perfectly good load of marijuana stacked out in a cow pasture eight miles north of Animas? Why had two Border Patrol cars and one county deputy driven right by them between the Valley View Church and the interstate and not recognized them? Probably the most confusing thing of all was the fact that Buster Saunders, the sheriff, had mentioned that authorities had been watching the pickup that was stuck in the mud below Birch Springs for several days.

These things and a thousand others had consumed Ben's thoughts all of his waking hours. They consumed the conversations he, Caroline and Tamara shared. And now the state police were calling, wanting to ask him a few questions. At this point Ben considered the state police to be his friends. He needed a friend. A whole bunch of them would be better. Yes, he told Tamara, he would talk to them.

Tamara, Caroline, and Ben arrived at the New Mexico State Police office at 10:00 a.m. The officers asked to speak to Caroline and Tamara first, and they ushered them into a room and left Ben sitting in the lobby looking at magazines. After a few minutes, Caroline and Tamara reemerged with several officers. Ben had no idea what his wife and daughter had been asked or what their answers had been.

Ben was then asked to follow the officers. He was led down a hallway and into a small conference room by two officers from the New Mexico State Police and a woman wearing a business suit. She introduced herself as Celia, stating that she was an investigator for the FBI. The two state policemen and the FBI agent were polite but very businesslike. They offered Ben a seat next to a long table and told him to relax while they made themselves ready. They got into their briefcases and extracted voice recorders. Ben immediately stood up and told them that he would not talk to them if they were going to record the interview.

"Mr. Moody," one of the state policemen said, "this is only usual procedure in these types of situations. Really, this is quite harmless."

"Surely you trust us, Mr. Moody. We are only trying to get to the bottom of this whole affair," Celia said while staring at him coldly. Ben noticed that she stood about five feet eight and was athletic and trim. She could have been called attractive if she hadn't been so cold. He imagined that she might have a black leather braided whip stuffed down the leg of her business suit. He was sure she knew how to use it.

"I don't trust anyone right now," Ben told them. The three officers stared at him for a moment, and then they put away their recording devices. He would eventually learn that it didn't matter anyway. The room was wired with hidden microphones as well as cameras. The voice recorder act was a test to see how he would react.

The officers sat down and told Ben, "You can trust us. We are here to help you. We are public servants. Tell us, Mr. Moody, where exactly did this happen?"

"I had been working on some roads and stock tanks near Birch Springs, which is on the southeast side of Animas Peak. By the road it's close to fifty miles south of Animas. As the crow flies it's probably only thirty miles or thereabouts. You go through San Luis Pass, which is on the Continental Divide, and then turn back north a few miles. I drove in there to work on my machine, and right there at Birch Springs, I saw a pickup sitting in the bottom of the creek like it was stuck. It had what I thought was marijuana in it and some laying on the ground. I knew what it was, and it spooked me, and I turned around and started back out of there."

"You were alarmed?" Celia asked.

"Yeah, I didn't want to get mixed up in some kind of drug deal," Ben answered.

"So, have you been mixed up in drug deals before?" Celia asked.

"No! But there is a lot of drugs coming up through there, and I didn't want to be involved."

"Are there other local people, friends of yours, who are involved?" Celia asked. It was now obvious to Ben that she was running this show.

"I don't know who is involved; I just knew I wanted outa there! And I tried to leave."

"Tell us what happened next."

"I tried to drive back out the way I had driven in, and I was stopped by the Mexicans. The ones who had been with the pickup that I had seen stuck in the mud down in the creek below Birch Springs. They jerked me out of my truck and tied my hands and blindfolded me, and we went back down to where the truck was stuck. They kept me there all day while they were doing something with the truck. There was lots of trucks coming and going. I think some of the people there were Americans."

"Why do you think that?"

"Because of their phony accents."

"Phony accents? Really? Were they speaking Spanish or English?"

"Spanish,"

"Do you speak Spanish, Mr. Moody?" Celia asked.

"No, a little, but not very well."

"Then how can you be sure they were phony?"

"I can't. But I think there were some American citizens there," Ben said. The two state policemen and Celia looked at each other with no expression.

"So, what happened at the end of the day?" Celia continued to ask all of the questions.

"We all got in the pickups and started driving out of there. At one point they told me they were taking me into

Mexico, but I think that was a lie because we never got near the border."

"How do you know if you were blindfolded?"

"Because before long they got lost, and they took my blindfold off and told me to tell them where to go."

"So you helped them." It was more of a statement coming out of Celia's mouth, rather than a question.

"There was ten or twelve of them and one of me. My hands were tied. They had guns! Yeah, I helped them. What was I supposed to do?"

"Where did you go?" Celia continued.

"We ended up on the Deer Creek Road and turned north toward the OK Bar and the Adobes and the XT. All of this is on the east side of the mountain."

"And eventually you made it to Animas?"

"Yes."

"How did you go through all of those people's property?"

"It's all owned by one ranch."

"What? You drove forty or fifty miles from where you started until you reached Animas! There's no way one person or one ranch could own that much property! How did you get permission to drive through that many people's property?" Celia demanded.

"It's all owned by one ranch, Las Animas Ranch. All of it, owned by one family."

"No one can own that much property!"

"Well, it is, whether you believe it or not." Ben said. "Look, I can take you down there. I'll be glad to, and I can show you exactly where and how we went."

"Oh, no!" One of the men from the state police finally spoke, "That is an unsafe zone. We are not going down there."

Ben paused and looked at the three law enforcement officers, two state policemen and an FBI agent. He couldn't believe what he had just heard. "Is that area in the United States?"

"What is that supposed to mean? That area has been designated as unsafe. You still haven't explained how you traversed through all of that land and how you dealt with trespassing on private property." Celia spat.

Ben remembered seeing a large topographical map on the wall out in the hallway. He suggested they step out into the hallway where he could show them on the map the roads they had taken. When they all were standing close to the map, Ben took his forefinger and began tracing the route he and the Narcos had traveled a few hours earlier.

"So who owns all of that land?" Celia demanded for the third time.

"One family owns it. The whole thing is called Las Animas Ranch. They own hundreds and hundreds of square miles of land," Ben explained again.

"There is no way one person could own that much land!" Celia just could not get past the concept of a huge cattle ranch being owned by one person or one family.

As they all stood staring at the map with Celia trying to process the information Ben was giving her, a man that Ben had not seen before walked out into the hallway. He was wearing a gun belt complete with an automatic pistol, extra ammunition clips, and gadgets of different types hanging from the gun belt. "You are a liar!" he said abruptly to Ben.

"What?" Ben retorted in surprise.

"I said that you are a liar," the man repeated while the other three people who had been with Ben continually for a half hour stood looking at the man.

"How do you figure?" Ben asked.

"People don't load drugs with masks on."

Ben looked at the man in astonishment. *Where had he come from. Was he actually part of the questioning process?* The man raved on "You said they were loading drugs with masks on."

"I never said anyone was loading drugs with masks on."

"Well that's what the records are showing."

"What records are you talking about? Where did you hear that I had said someone was loading drugs with a mask on? Or did someone else say that?"

"The records show that you said people were loading drugs with masks on!" The officer was now very loud, almost screaming into Ben's face.

Tamara heard the man's loud and obnoxious voice from the room where she and Caroline were waiting for Ben's interview to be over. She came around the corner and stuck a finger into the officer's face, "Back off right now, big shot! Has someone been arrested here? Do you have a warrant for this man's arrest?" She pointed at her father and then went on with her index finger only inches from the man's face. "If you have a warrant have you read him his Miranda rights? Have you shown my father your badge and identification?" She had backed the man against the wall and seemed more than willing to scratch his eyes out. The man looked at her, seething with anger as he did so, while the other two state policemen and Celia, the FBI agent, looked on with a noncommittal, even casual, look on their faces. The man squeezed by Tamara's fingertip and left the room without saying anymore.

"We would like to see your wife's phone," one of the officers said to Ben.

"Why do you want my wife's phone?"

"We want to see who she talked to while you were missing."

Ben borrowed Tamara's cell phone because he had not been given his phone back, if the authorities had it which he figured they did, but actually he had not seen it since the outlaws had hidden it along with his lunchbox and wallet while they had been parked and hiding behind the XT shipping corrals early in the morning the day before. He called Sheriff Saunders and said, "Buster, this is Ben Moody. The state police and FBI want to see Caroline's cell phone. I don't particularly want to give it to them. What should I do?"

"Well," Buster said, "you can either give it to them or they can get a subpoena and get it. Either way, they will get it if they want it."

An officer spoke to Ben while he hung up from his call to Buster, "We just want to check out some of the phone numbers on it. It will only take a few minutes, and then we will give it back." Caroline handed the officer her cell phone and he walked down the hallway and into a room. Ben, Caroline, and Tamara continued to stand in the hall and within five minutes the man came back and returned the phone. With that accomplished the state patrolmen and Celia seemed to lose interest in any more conversation. Relieved, the Moody family left the office building and went back to Tamara's house.

Chapter Twelve
January 12, 2016
11:00 a.m.

Jim Yarbrough sat at his kitchen table contemplating the meeting that was about to take place right there at the table where he sat. He had made coffee and had placed three cups on the table indicating the number of people that were supposed to be present when the fireworks started. Of course he had no way of knowing there would be any fireworks, but he suspected there would be. He had been through meetings like this before and usually there were fireworks, or at least a little smoke.

Jim Yarbrough had been vocal about Ben Moody's kidnapping, that is to say he had told numerous people what he thought. The word on the street was that the Border Patrol thought Ben Moody was dirty. The officials believed the kidnapping was nothing but a ruse created to make it look like Ben was not involved when, in fact, he had actually shown up at the correct time to help get the drugs out of the truck that was stuck in the mud and into his vehicle and then guided the Mexicans north, and afterward turned himself into a victim. Jim Yarbrough was mad.

Having a mad rancher, or any other kind of civilian that was mad, was not something the Border Patrol lost much sleep over. After all, they were a government agency.

They were hard at work risking their lives on a daily basis protecting Middle America from being invaded by illegal aliens, drug lords, Islamic terrorists, and a host of other dangerous threats including a smorgasbord of life-threatening diseases any or all of the intruders might be carrying when they enter the United States. Using the obligations and importance of their hazy mission statement coupled with a policy of never giving much information to anyone, especially the media, the U.S. Border Patrol considered itself to be untouchable and above reproach.

Jim Yarbrough was the fly in the ointment. To some he was an enigma, very hard to figure out; but to many he was a problem. The Border Patrol had an ongoing program to discredit him and make him look crazy. To some watching, it seemed the Border Patrol had an easy job doing that.

When a neighboring rancher had been murdered by a Narco scout several years earlier, Jim Yarbrough had gone viral, speaking about the United States government's failure to protect its citizen. He had been interviewed by numerous major television networks. He had been interviewed by a host of major newspapers including the *New York Times*, the *Washington Post*, the *Los Angeles Times*, as well as the *Asahi Shinebun* from Japan and the *Guardian* from the United Kingdom. His story had always been the same: The United States government and its agency, the U.S. Border Patrol, were derelict in their duty to protect the citizens of their country.

When a Border Patrol agent was murdered by Narco mules in an ambush west of Douglas a few miles, the Border Patrol lied about it and reported that the agent had been killed by friendly fire and said there were no Mexican outlaws anywhere around. Jim Yarbrough, with the help of an experienced investigative reporter from Illinois had uncovered evidence supporting the fact that the agent had been in a gun battle with Narcos. The reporter had written a book about the whole affair which was very embarrassing to the government, especially the Border Patrol.

Jim Yarbrough told people that the Border Patrol had tried to frame him by sending an agent disguised as a Mexican hauling drugs up to Jim's ranch, and when Jim had confronted the agent disguised as a Mexican, the agent had offered to sell Jim a backpack full of marijuana. The disguise, or trick, hadn't worked. The Border Patrol had a very large dossier containing every fact they had ever been able to collect on Jim Yarbrough. They hated him and he felt the same about them.

Jim had received a phone call on January 11 from a Border Patrol agent from the Lordsburg station by the name of Kent Smith. Kent and Jim were acquainted, having seen each other out in the field on numerous occasions as well as several unplanned meetings they had experienced at a local gun store. Their meetings had always been congenial, perhaps even friendly. Agent Smith was on the Horse Patrol unit from the Lordsburg station and loved to tell Jim horse training stories. Jim Yarbrough thought that Smith was a gunsel who didn't know his head from a hole in the ground but got a kick out of listening to the agent tell stories. When Agent Smith called he told Jim that he would like to have a meeting with him. Soon.

"What about?" Jim Yarbrough asked.

"We need to talk about Ben Moody," Agent Smith said.

"What about him? What's there to talk about?"

"Look—they've asked me to come and talk some sense into you. Maybe give you some facts you are not aware of. They've asked me to come because I'm the only one who can get along with you."

Jim Yarbrough laughed out loud until he sent himself into a coughing fit. When he finally caught his breath he asked, "So when is this going to happen?"

"How about tomorrow about eleven thirty?"

"Who's coming?"

"Just me. Nobody else wants to." Agent Smith chuckled loud enough to be heard when he said that.

Jim Yarbrough had been in many meetings with high-level Border Patrol agents. He had attended a meeting with the secretary of Homeland Security in which the few guests present had undergone a thorough background check by the Secret Service. He had been in numerous meetings with United States senators and congressmen. He had been to the East Coast on two occasions to speak about border issues including one trip to Washington DC where he had been part of a delegation to speak at a Federation of Immigration Reform conference. When it came to meetings, he was no amateur. He knew the Border Patrol had some kind of agenda they wanted to promote, and they were using Agent Smith to accomplish it, and because of his experience, he decided that he needed a credible witness that he could trust. He called his Cochise County deputy sheriff friend, Mark Ferrell, and asked him if he would drive down to his ranch and sit in on the meeting with Border Patrol agent Kent Smith. Mark Ferrell agreed to meet him at the ranch at eleven thirty the following day.

Deputy Ferrell drove into the ranch the next morning, January 12, at 11:00 a.m., which was a half hour early. Jim invited him into the house and told him that he really didn't want the deputy to do or say anything. "Just sit here and listen to everything that is said by me and the Border Patrol agent. I just want you to be a witness."

"Okay, that's what I'll do," the deputy replied, and he and Jim visited for about thirty minutes until the Border Patrol agent, Kent Smith, pulled into the ranch and parked right next to the deputy's vehicle.

As Deputy Ferrell sat and waited at the kitchen table, Jim Yarbrough walked outside and shook Agent Smith's hand and invited him in the house. They walked in the front door, and the Border Patrol agent looked at the deputy sitting a few feet away at the kitchen table. "Kent, you probably know Deputy Ferrell from the Cochise County sheriff's office, don't you?"

"Yes, I think we've met."

Deputy Ferrell stood up, and the two men shook hands. "I asked Deputy Ferrell to come and sit in on the meeting. I didn't figure you cared," Jim Yarbrough said.

"No! Of course not," Agent Smith replied.

Jim poured everyone a cup of coffee, and for a minute or so they sat in silence. It was obvious, or so Jim Yarbrough thought, that the Border Patrol agent had not planned on a deputy or anyone else being present during the meeting. Jim knew that this development had thrown the Border Patrol agent off balance, and that was just what he wanted.

"So what's on your mind, Kent?" Jim asked.

"Well, like I told you yesterday on the phone, they wanted me to come and talk to you about this situation with Ben Moody."

"Who are - they?" Jim asked.

"Don Edsel, the patrol agent in charge at the Douglas station."

"Don Edsel! What's he got to do with it? The kidnapping took place in Hidalgo County in the Lordsburg station's country. Heck, the Douglas station is part of the Tucson Sector. But Lordsburg is part of the El Paso Sector. Why would Don Edsel be concerned about Lordsburg's business? What have I got to do with it? Why do they want you to talk to me?" Jim said.

The Border Patrol agent was silent for a moment. He looked as if he was searching for the correct words. He looked at the deputy who stared back at him in silence. The Border Patrol agent was wary, wondering how to proceed. "Well," he said, "you've been making a lot of noise - "

"And the Border Patrol wants me to shut up!"

"It's not like that, but - "

"What's it like then?" Jim Yarbrough demanded.

"It didn't happen like you are telling people it happened. You don't know the whole story."

"Really? What exactly have I been saying?" Jim asked.

"Well, it wasn't a kidnapping. Ben Moody may not have been abducted like you are telling people. It may not have been like you think it was," the agent said.

"Ben Moody was held captive for over a day, and he was taken across state lines, which should make it a federal offence; and now you're saying he wasn't kidnapped?"

"We think he may have been part of it."

"You think Ben Moody is working for the Mexican drug cartel?" Jim had now raised his voice considerable, and he was leaned forward as if he was ready to pounce on top of Border Patrol agent Smith, who was leaning back in his chair trying to keep himself separated from the rancher, Jim Yarbrough; the same one some people called notorious or even a little crazy? Cochise County deputy Mark Ferrell sat in his chair in total silence and did not appear to have taken sides or to have an opinion.

"We think there is a chance things are not what you think they are," the agent said again.

"Let me tell you something, Kent; Ben Moody sure as hell isn't working for the drug cartel, and you can tell your dumbass friend Don Edsel that I said so."

"That's fine, if that's your opinion, that's fine. But you ought to get your facts straight; that's all the Border Patrol wants. They want you to get your facts straight."

"What facts do I have wrong?"

"Well, you know that there are a lot of dirty ranchers, and we think he may be one of them."

"Who's dirty? " Jim came out of his chair and slammed his fist down on the table in front of Agent Smith. "You think you know so damn much! Give me the name of one legitimate cattle rancher between Columbus and Douglas and tell me they're corrupt! Name one, bigshot! Name one!" Jim was now talking very loud, some would say he was shouting and spitting. The deputy sat silently watching. Jim continued, "Give me one name of a corrupt cattle rancher between Columbus, New Mexico and Douglas, Arizona. I know all of them, and I'm saying they are not corrupt. Name one!"

"I can't name one, but we know they are there," Agent Smith muttered.

"You guys want to make everyone think all the ranchers along the border are working for the cartel, but you have no evidence. You cannot produce any facts, but you promote that agenda. If we are all so corrupt, why don't you arrest us?"

"I'm not saying everyone is corrupt! But we think Ben Moody might have been part of it. They want you to consider that possibility. That's why they sent me to talk to you. They want you to wait and see what happens."

Jim Yarbrough came out of his chair again slamming his fist down on the table. The Border Patrol agent's coffee cup bounced on top of the heavy table. Border Patrol agent Smith backed his chair away from the table and stood up, taking a step backward as he did so. "Look," he was also getting loud, "I didn't come down here to get screamed at! I'm only doing what I'm told. I thought we were friends, but I can see now that I was mistaken."

"Let me tell you something, Mr. Smith, Ben Moody is a friend of mine. And he is not working for the drug cartel, and as far as I'm concerned, you and old Don Edsel need your ass kicked for spreading rumors about him."

"Well," Agent Smith said as he walked toward the front door, "I will just leave then. I can see that it's impossible to have a friendly conversation with you."

"Don't let the screen door hit you in the ass when you leave," Jim Yarbrough said.

Deputy Ferrell causally picked up his cup and took a sip of coffee. He hadn't spoken a word throughout the short conversation.

Chapter Thirteen
January 13, 2016

After spending five nights at Tamara's place in Deming trying to rest and get over the ordeal that Ben and his entire family had been through beginning on January 7, Ben and Caroline returned to their home at Animas with plans to start life all over again. Ben was having some trouble sleeping but had not had any nightmares. He was mentally and physically drained but felt a little better every day. Emotionally he was stressed about the numerous, subtle threats the Mexicans had made to him in the hours that he had been with them. He was mainly stressed about their obvious knowledge of his family: They knew where he lived, where he worked, his lifestyle; but the thing that bothered him the most was the phone call his Mexican companion had received as they were traveling down Interstate 10 in route to Willcox when someone had told the Mexican in the truck with him, "Tell him to tell his wife to go home . . ."

How did someone who was connected to his kidnappers know that Caroline had left the house? Who was the connection and why were they connected to the man who was directing him to drive to Willcox.

Ben and Caroline had gone over this puzzle a thousand times, all the while Caroline trying to remember if she had seen or talked to anyone besides the county sheriff, her children, and Betty Davis. The rabbit trails that her mind would take her down while she tried to remember everything that had happened on that night when Ben was missing always ended up focused on the Border Patrol vehicles and the charcoal-colored Suburban that had lurked about her driveway on the morning of January 8. But she had no proof whether those vehicles were the missing piece of the puzzle or not. There were so many things that didn't make any sense.

When they got to Animas, Ben was able to meet with Tommy Davis for the first time other than the brief encounter at the community center where Ben had given the various law enforcement agencies the interview they had thought they needed before he even had time to realize that he was free and safe—maybe.

The two men told each other their separate sides of the same story, and Ben heard in detail for the first time how Tommy and Junior had tracked the Narco caravan through the mud and snow around the east side of Animas Mountain, passing the OK Bar, the Adobes Camp, and finally reaching the Cloverdale Road. By comparing notes and memories, they finally agreed that the jefe's orders for the caravan to leave the main road and hide out behind the big set of shipping corrals near the XT was done so Tommy and Junior could drive by the Narcos and get ahead of them. Tommy realized, in hindsight, that the ground at the XT corrals had dried out too much by the time they reached that point and caused him to miss the caravan's tracks when they left the road. There had also been a considerable amount of vehicle tracks made by the XT camp man, making the tracking process more difficult. Both men puzzled over the fact that the Border Patrol had moved their radar unit that had been parked there for months and had chosen that very day to do it.

Tommy gave Ben an update on what had happened in the previous days at Birch Springs: He, Tommy, had driven down there the day after Ben had returned safe and sound to Animas in an attempt to retrieve all of Ben's tools that had been scattered out all over what had become a crime scene.

When Tommy arrived on January 9, there were several Border Patrol trucks present at the site as well as several other unmarked vehicles. Yellow caution tape had been strung up around the entire area, and numerous men were either walking around as if they were looking for something or standing and visiting. Tommy had requested, talking to a Border Patrol agent, that he be allowed to collect all of Ben Moody's tools. He was told that the entire area was classified as a crime scene and nothing could be removed. The agent advised him to come back the next day and perhaps the situation would be different.

The next day Tommy returned and found vehicles parked and men acting as if they were looking for something. The yellow tape was still in place. This time Tommy talked to a man in plain clothes who introduced himself as an FBI agent and was told that the investigation was ongoing and the tools could not be released. The man suggested that Tommy might try again the next day.

The third day when Tommy arrived there was only one Border Patrol agent and a Hidalgo County deputy, and they were in the process of taking the yellow tape down. They gave Tommy permission to pick up the tools that had been taken out of Ben's pickup. Tommy and Junior, who had accompanied him, spent several hours picking up the tools that were scattered about over several acres. They walked a tight grid pattern, searching, putting a lot of effort into their attempt to leave nothing behind. In the end about half of the tools were not found and were never accounted for. Most of the tools that were missing were expensive electric hand tools such as drills, saws, and other similar implements. The value of the missing tools was between four and five thousand dollars. Mexican drug runners do not usually deal in second-hand tools. American citizens are more likely to be interested in those things.

Chapter Fourteen
January 15, 2016

After a week had passed since Ben Moody's abduction, the rumor mill in Hidalgo County was running at full throttle. Little of it made its way back to Ben and Caroline directly because the people who thought they knew everything were best at talking behind the Moodys' backs. But some of the gossip did make its way to them, and most of what they heard was negative.

Back at work for Tommy Davis, Ben went southeast of Animas a dozen miles and looked at a dam and reservoir that needed repaired with a bulldozer. The woman who owned the cattle ranch told Ben about one of the rumors that was being told. The lady rancher was a newcomer to the area, having owned and lived on her ranch for about ten years. She was an unusual example of a southwestern rancher because of living in New York City for a number of years and in Israel before that. She was quite sophisticated and cosmopolitan yet had adjusted to the ranching business with enthusiasm. She was also nobody's fool. She told Ben that a woman, a native of Hidalgo County who was a county commissioner, had informed her that Ben was guilty of cooperating with the Narcos and had been working for them for a long time. He was, in her opinion, "Guilty as hell." The newly transplanted New Yorker told Ben this story with a grin on her face. At first it made Ben mad, and then he realized that the rancher didn't believe a word of it and thought the commissioner was a gossip and rumor monger and definitely full of crap! She hinted to Ben that he needed to lighten up—nobody with any brains thought he was guilty of cooperating with Mexican outlaws.

Because of her job working for the district attorney's office in Deming, Tamara was familiar with the legal system and its many facets and its different services. Through research and conversations with several people connected to the district attorney's office and the New Mexico State Police, she became aware of the services available from a victims' rights' advocate, who actually was an employee of the FBI; and Tamara made an appointment to meet with the advocate to discuss her dad's case. Tamara recognized that Ben was suffering from some degree of post-traumatic stress disorder, and it seemed that law enforcement officials from all agencies had an accusatory attitude and dialogue during all of their interviews with Ben. And yet, at the same time, no charges had been filed or warrants issued and served. Any comments or accusations that had been made to Ben had been subtle and unprofessional; or at least that was Tamara's opinion.

Tamara walked into the victim advocate's office, and the lady FBI agent asked her exactly what was on her mind. Tamara proceeded to explain that her parents had both suffered from Ben's kidnapping experience. He had been threatened by the drug runners, had lost several thousand dollars' worth of his own equipment during the event, and since then had been treated badly by the authorities. Tamara told the agent that in her opinion her father was a victim, and he had received no justice. Could she help?

The victims' advocate looked at Tamara and said, "Ben Moody is not a victim. In fact, he is guilty of conspiring to traffic illegal narcotics with illegal aliens who are known outlaws; and he, Ben Moody, will soon be charged." And with that statement, the lady FBI agent made it plain that the conversation was over, and Tamara walked out.

The same day that Tamara requested help from the FBI's victims' advocate in Deming, Ben received a call from the state police asking him to meet with them again at the Animas Community Center for another interview, which would be the third time he had answered questions coming from several agencies. They also asked if he would bring his son Rocky. Ben agreed to meet with them at 1:00 p.m.

Present at the meeting and representing the government were an investigator from the New Mexico State Police and Celia, the FBI agent who had interviewed Ben in Deming, as well as another state policeman. No one else was present.

The three law officers were there at the community center and waiting for Ben and Rocky when they arrived. Everyone said hello in a congenial manner, and then Rocky was asked to stay outside, so Ben walked into the metal building alone. Ben was offered a chair next to a long metal folding table, the type that would be used for a family picnic. The building was cold even though a large heater had been turned on. The cement floor and the walls of the building, which were made of sheet metal, created an even colder and uninviting atmosphere. It was three against one, and therefore a very lopsided affair. The investigator for the state police opened up the interrogation.

"So when you got to Willcox, they dropped you off at the truck stop?"

Ben's eyes opened up very wide when he heard that. "How did you know they let me off at the truck stop? I have never told anyone I was dropped off at the truck stop?"

"Well, we just heard that you were dropped off at the truck stop."

"Oh, yeah? Where did you hear I was dropped off at the truck stop? I have never told anyone that I was dropped off at the truck stop. Who told you?"

"We just heard it. It really doesn't matter," the lawman said.

"What truck stop was it?" Ben asked the state policeman.

"It was the TA, the only truck stop in town," the lawman said.

"Actually there are three truck stops in town. How did you know I was turned loose at the TA?"

"We just figured it was the TA because that's where we always stop when we go through town."

Ben stared at the lawman. *They were there watching me,* Ben thought. *What the hell is going on?*

Celia, the FBI agent, came at him from another angle, "You have numbers on your cell phone contact list that belong to known drug dealers. Do you talk to these people often? Why do you talk to these people?"

"Where did you get my phone?"

"It was given to us by the sheriff. It was found out in the desert, and you have known drug dealers in your contact list. Why do you talk to these people?" Celia repeated her question.

"You need to explain to us why you are talking to drug dealers," the state investigator chimed in.

"I do a lot of work for a lot of people all over the county. When someone asks me or Tommy Davis to come and put in a new septic system or a new pipeline or dig a hole with some equipment, we don't ask them if they are drug dealers. We do that kind of work for people all over the place, and I'm sure that some of them might be drug dealers, but it's not our job to ask people what they do for a living. That's your job, not mine. So I probably do have some drug dealers' numbers in my phone. So what?"

"We found your fingerprints all over bales of dope; we know you were helping bring dope north!" the state investigator said.

"I bet you did find my fingerprints on some bales of marijuana. They made me sit on it in the pickup for hours! My head was jammed up into the ceiling of the pickup because they had dope stacked underneath me. I was made to help unload a truckload of marijuana out in a cow pasture eight or ten miles north of here, so I'm sure I put lots of fingerprints on that dope, too!"

"If you weren't helping move the dope north, as you claim you weren't, why did you help?" Celia interjected.

"The fact that my hands were tied, and the man I was with had a gun might have had something to do with it."

"We think you are involved in the drug trade. You've made several large deposits in the bank in the last several months. Where did that money come from?" Celia asked.

"Do you call $30,000 a large deposit? That won't even buy a new pickup! I weaned and sold my calves in November. I also sold a dozen old cull cows. That's the only deposits of any size I've made in the last year. How do you know how much money I've put in the bank anyway? What business is it to you?" Ben questioned.

"We have ways of finding out." Celia answered.

"Really?" Ben said. "Did you ask the bank what I did with most of that 30,000? Did you ask them how much of my note I paid off? Have you found out what my personal pickup is worth? I guarantee you it's not worth 30,000. It is seven years old and has 140,000 miles on it."

Celia looked at him coldly. The investigator for the state police drummed the tabletop with his fingers. "Look," he said, "we can prove you communicate with known drug dealers, you and Tommy Davis both; you have money, you lead an unusual lifestyle, you got connected with what was probably the biggest caravan of narcotics to ever come through Hidalgo County. We know you are dirty." He paused and gave Ben a stern look. "We know all of you ranchers south of I-10 are dirty. It would be easier on you if you would help us."

Everyone in the room became quiet, and for a moment the law officers seemed to have run out of ideas, and then the investigator for the state police told Ben, "We are going to bring your son in now. We would appreciate your cooperation and ask you to remain silent while we question him."

Ben stayed quiet and just stared at them while the other state policeman, who up to this point had said nothing, went to the door and asked Rocky to come in. They motioned him to a chair next to a different table from the one Ben sat at, and Rocky sat down. The investigator for the state police spoke, "We have further evidence that your father has been facilitating the trafficking of drugs. As a result of this evidence, your father is soon going to be charged."

"Why didn't you guys rescue my dad when he was in Willcox?" Rocky was almost shouting as he said the words. He had been standing close to the door as he waited outside of the building and had heard everything that had been said before he was asked to come in.

"We didn't know it was a hostage situation," the state police inspector said.

"So, you were there watching when my dad was turned loose at the TA. You just admitted it!" Now Rocky was screaming. His face was red.

"I didn't say we were there watching."

"Then how did you know he was turned loose at the truck stop? He never told anybody."

"We know but, like other ranchers in the area, your father is working with drug cartels. It would help your father's case if you would cooperate with us."

"Yeah right! My dad is in the drug business. That's exactly why he drives a worn out pickup, lives in an old ranch house that needs remodeled, and, at the age of sixty-five, he's still working his ass off every day. That makes a lot of sense. You guys are desperate to catch a criminal, but you can't. You couldn't catch a fart with a vacuum cleaner!"

The lawmen turned their backs on Rocky and directed their attention back to Ben, "Why did the men you were riding with tell you they were going to stay with you and your family for a while?"

"You tell me. I wondered that myself," Ben said wondering how the investigators knew the Mexicans had told him that very thing.

"Did they tell you they were taking you down into Mexico?" Celia asked.

"At one point they did, yes," Ben replied.

"Why did you decide to go to the TA truck stop?"

Ben stared at her in unbelief. He couldn't believe what he was hearing. He paused for a few moments trying to gather his thoughts while everyone in the room looked at him. Finally he said, "Well, I guess I'm going to have to tell you the truth. There were really two men with me, and they ordered me to go out on a dirt road several miles out of town where we met another truck load of outlaws, and I turned the Mexicans loose there, and then I drove off."

"That's not what you told us a while ago!" Celia said while pointing her index finger at him in an accusatory fashion.

"Well," Ben answered slowly, "what I told you a while ago was the truth, and this is a lie. But you seem to want to deal in lies, so I thought a lie would make you happy. I'm having trouble figuring out what you people want."

"We would like to get to the bottom of this!" Celia hissed. She turned toward her two colleagues and said, "I don't think we are making any headway here today. It's time we ended this and go back to Deming." She started gathering up her baggage.

"Are you through with us?" Ben asked.

"Yes, but you will be hearing from us again," Celia answered, so Ben and Rocky made their exit.

That night Ben and Caroline talked over the day's events as well as everything that had transpired in the last week or so. There were so many things that didn't fit. "Can you remember saying anything to anyone that I was being taken to Willcox?"

"No," Caroline replied. "I never told anyone anything."

"So how did they know that I was going to Willcox?

How could they have been there watching when I dropped the Mexican off at the TA?" Ben said.

"Remember," Caroline said, "Buster mentioned to me later that he had called the Cochise County sheriff's office and told them that they had word you were headed to Willcox, and out of professional courtesy would they please leave you alone and allow you to return to Animas under your own power."

"They obviously didn't care anything about me or about catching the outlaw."

Buster's statement about asking the Cochise County sheriff's office to not intervene by trying to apprehend Ben Moody or the Narco smuggler that he was with didn't coincide very well with Jim Yarbrough's phone call to Cochise County deputy Mark Ferrell when he explained to the deputy about having a friend who had been kidnapped in Hidalgo County and turned loose in Willcox. Deputy Ferrell claimed that he knew nothing about it.

Chapter Fifteen
January 25, 2016

Uproar over Ben Moody's abduction became stronger throughout Hidalgo County and began to spread, especially through the cattle ranchers along the Mexican border in both New Mexico and Arizona. Although some locals—like the commissioner who told people Ben Moody was guilty of helping move drugs—said negative things about Ben, most of the ranchers thought Ben was a victim. All of them had experienced some degree of vandalism and life-threatening situations because of illegal alien traffic, but also, some had felt uncomfortable with their relationship with federal authorities. There was a general feeling of distrust between the cattle ranching community and the Border Patrol. The Border Patrol thought they owned everything within seventy-five miles of the border and could do anything they wanted to, or so it seemed to some owners of large cattle ranches. Foremost in the ranchers' minds was the fact that, in spite of the millions of dollars of taxpayers' money that was being spent on border security, the tide wasn't turning; the aliens, including many Narcos, kept coming; and they were traveling across ranchers' land. The Border Patrol had intentionally tightened security in the border towns and pushed the illegal traffic out into the countryside. As a result of all of the first-hand knowledge and experiences cattle ranchers had dealing with alien traffic, they were very sympathetic with Ben Moody's predicament.

There were a few key people who refused to cave in to the rumors being spread that said Ben Moody was in some kind of partnership with Mexican drug traffickers. Chief among that crowd was Betty Davis. She began talking to another local woman named Raquel Nunez who had connections with the New Mexico Cattlegrowers' Association and had also been involved in organizing large meetings. They started talking about producing a community meeting: The type that had come to be known as town hall meetings, similar to ones that had been produced for national television during presidential elections or some other national event. Perhaps, if done correctly, the meeting could draw some attention from television stations and newspapers, and the truth about life on the border would be told. In spite of all the attention Ben Moody's kidnapping had received locally, there had been no coverage of the affair in any major newspaper or on any television news show either locally or nationally. Ben Moody had been taken across state lines which, or at least as local people thought, should have made it a federal case, but the media at every level had been silent, and there had been no reporting about what had happened. That fact was no surprise to many ranchers who had witnessed firsthand how the Department of Homeland Security had been successful at keeping violent crime created by illegal aliens out of the media's supply of news to report. There were other border horror stories that the general public had never heard. Betty and Raquel went on a mission to change all of that.

Raquel Nunez had represented Hidalgo County as well as a livestock video auction company at a New Mexico

Cattlegrowers' statewide meeting where she had spoken as a representative for both entities. While at Albuquerque at this event, she had become acquainted with Sheila Morris who was at that time the executive director for the New Mexico Cattlegrowers' Association, as well as an editor and publisher of several livestock trade publications. Sheila also had a lot of experience as a lobbyist for the New Mexico Cattlegrowers' Association. She was a native of Hidalgo County, having grown up on a cattle ranch near Cloverdale, south of Animas. After talking with Betty Davis and trying to come up with some kind of plan to produce a public meeting to raise awareness about the out-of-control situation on the Mexican border using Ben Moody as the meeting's main focus and talking point, Raquel suggested she talk to Sheila Morris, asking her for advice as well as requesting the support and involvement in the meeting from the cattle growers organization. Raquel told Sheila the Ben Moody story and explained how it seemed that government agencies were treating him as a suspect instead of a victim and that justice was not being served.

After listening to Raquel's narrative about Ben Moody and what was transpiring after his abduction, Sheila promised the cattle growers' support and offered assistance in both the planning and production of the meeting. She also said she would use her connections with state and national legislators to get them to attend and speak. Shelia, Raquel, and Betty all agreed that the meeting should be held at Animas, the epicenter of the Moody affair as well as the invasion of outlaw Narcos that had reached viral proportions. It was decided that the point man (or, in this case, woman) for planning the meeting would be Raquel, who was young, well educated, well spoken, and beautiful. They gave her the ball and she took off running.

They had a concept, a location, and some heavy duty support and now they had to decide what exactly their agenda would be. Who should they get to be guest speakers? Raquel called Jim Yarbrough the Arizona rancher who had tried to get the Cochise County sheriff's office involved the day Ben Moody was turned loose and who, subsequently, had driven Border Patrol agent Kent Smith out of his house for what he felt were false accusations about Ben Moody. Raquel and her husband were friends with Jim and his wife. She knew that Jim Yarbrough, whom federal agents called El Loco because of his ferocious defense of victimized American citizens, had been to many meetings with senators and congressmen discussing the out-of-control situation on the border. She knew that Jim had been on television news shows and had been quoted in major newspapers discussing border issues, and he had done a considerable amount of public speaking about the subject. She asked Jim for advice about the meeting.

"If you want to have a meeting that has any meaning and that people will appreciate, don't let any politicians or federal agents talk. I've been to a hundred meetings with senators, and congressmen, and Border Patrol sector chiefs and have been to one meeting with the secretary of Homeland Security; and any time you meet with those bureaucrats and politicians, you end up getting nothing out of it. They are arrogant, they lie to you, and they treat everyone in a condescending manner. As far as I'm concerned, it is a total waste of time to listen to a politician or Border Patrol agent," Jim told her.

"Well, who should we get to speak then?" Raquel asked.

"Get some local people who know and understand the issues. People who are leaders in the community. People who you know will speak the truth and not water it down. Everyone is sick of politicians who speak out of both sides of their mouths. Try and get some media there. Invite every politician and upper-level Border Patrol official within 300 miles but make them sit there and listen to the people talk."

"Would you be willing to speak?" Raquel asked.

"Yeah, sure, but you may not like what I say. I'm going to tell them the truth. I'm going to tell them that the Border Patrol is not on the border and the government doesn't know who the hell is coming across here."

"Okay, you're on!" Raquel said.

"Do I have your word that you won't let the Border Patrol talk? Because if they do, I'm going to walk out. I'm not interested in being part of another dog-and-pony show."

So now Raquel had her first guest speaker. She went on asking people and ended up with six speakers, one of whom was a large animal veterinary who had done work for most of the ranchers in the area. He said he wanted to inform the public about dangerous diseases that illegal aliens were bringing across the border unchecked. Besides Jim Yarbrough, she got four other New Mexico ranchers who had numerous life-threatening experiences with Narco aliens that they had encountered out in remote places, similar to Ben Moody's experience. Every speaker was sympathetic to Ben Moody's incident and believed him to be innocent of any wrongdoing.

So plans about the big meeting moved forward. The school auditorium at the Animas school was acquired, and the list of guest speakers was solidified, including Congressman Earnest Dolittle from New Mexico's

2nd Congressional District, whom Sheila Morris from the cattle growers insisted on inviting in spite of Jim Yarbrough's opinion. Raquel talked Jim into staying on board even though he had said he wouldn't attend if any politicians were allowed to speak. Every patrol agent in charge at every Border Patrol station in both the Tucson Sector as well as the El Paso Sector received a personal invitation to attend the meeting. But it was agreed on by Sheila, Betty, and Raquel that no federal agents would be allowed to speak. The word was spread around through every available channel that could be thought of, and the public was invited to come.

Congressman Dolittle arrived early in the afternoon, and Tommy and Betty Davis arranged for him to meet and listen to Ben Moody's story firsthand from Ben himself. He sat and listened for about an hour while Ben told him the whole story from the time he drove into Birch Springs and saw the pickup load of dope stuck in the mud until he was finally turned loose at the TA truck stop in Willcox and then made it back home to Animas. The congressman listened to the story but said almost nothing. Ben felt like he was talking to someone who wanted to be somewhere else.

When Ben finished his narrative, the congressman stood up and said he "would look into it" and then said he needed to leave and get ready for the meeting. As the congressman left the room, Tommy Davis came in. The two friends shook hands, and after pleasantries were exchanged, Tommy asked Ben if he and Caroline intended on attending the meeting. "Well, we haven't decided. We kinda feel like maybe it would be better if we didn't."

"I agree," Tommy said. "I'm not going to tell you not to come, but if you are there it might put the focus on you rather than on the bigger picture and what we are trying to accomplish. A lot of bad stuff has happened around here for years because of the government's inability to secure the border. This is just one more bad event in a long list of bad events. That's the message we are trying to send out to all who will listen."

"Okay, maybe it's best if we stay home, so that's what we will do," Ben replied.

Although Ben Moody's kidnapping had not been given any media coverage by any local or national television news shows and had not been written about in a single article in any local or national newspaper, the word about the town hall meeting in Animas had spread like wildfire. The meeting that was scheduled to start at 6:30 p.m. on a Tuesday evening drew an audience from six states, and by four in the afternoon, cars and pickup trucks started rolling into town. School was in session, so everyone who had come early had a hard time finding somewhere to park because on school days the parking lot was full of vehicles belonging to teenagers in school, teachers, and bus drivers. Strangers in unknown cars were parked alongside the roads and streets. The local café was closed, as usual, so visitors from out of town had nowhere to congregate, so they sat in their cars wherever they parked; and then when the school kids and faculty emptied the parking lot, it was soon refilled with people wanting to attend the meeting.

The school auditorium, which was a very nice facility, seated about 320 people, and it was full by a quarter to six. They opened up a partition that was between the auditorium and the cafeteria and sat chairs up in there, and by a quarter past six that was full also. People were standing against the walls. The final count was estimated that at least 650 were in attendance, although no one really knew if that was accurate.

The place was buzzing with Border Patrol agents in green uniforms, some of which were from the Tucson Sector and some from the El Paso Sector. El Paso's sector chief was there and walked in with his bombshell personal secretary and advisor who resembled Farrah Fawcett but, according to some opinions, was shaped better. They seated themselves three rows from the front and in the center. Soon other agents in green uniforms surrounded them and sat down.

Raquel Nunez was scheduled to be the emcee, and promptly at 6:30 she called the meeting to order. She had officiated at meetings before and knew how to control a crowd. Those who knew her would have said she was conservative, but she was very gracious and composed and could get up in front of a crowd without giving away her political persuasions. She asked a well-known rancher from Eddy County, 300 miles away, to stand and open the meeting with a prayer. Then she led everyone in the Pledge of Allegiance to the Flag and then a local gal who could sing belted out the national anthem, and did it justice.

Standing behind a podium, Raquel spoke into the microphone and addressed the crowd, "Good evening everyone. Thank you for coming. I want to thank the New Mexico Cattle Growers' Association for sponsoring this event, and I especially want to thank Sheila Morris of the cattle growers who put a tremendous effort into making this happen. We want to recognize the honorable Earnest Dolittle, New Mexico's congressman from the 2nd Congressional District who is here tonight and will speak to us at the end of the meeting. We have reached out to the offices of all of New Mexico and Arizona's senators and congressmen and requested their attendance, as well as the governors of both states. We have representatives here tonight from several of those offices. We also have a number of Border Patrol agents with us and want to welcome them.

The crowd, up to this point, was calm and quiet; and Raquel introduced the guest speakers and asked them to come to the stage where chairs had been set up for them to sit in while they waited their turn to speak. Raquel introduced the first speaker, Trudy Hess, a New Mexico rancher whose husband had been murdered by an illegal alien Narco while checking cattle in one of his pastures several years earlier. Unlike Ben Moody's kidnapping, Richard Hess had received a great deal of media coverage. Trudy spoke into the microphone, "Since my husband was killed, there have been thirty other American citizens die as a result of violence on the border coming from illegal alien traffic. It is all relative until it's your relative who's been killed. Then all of a sudden it gets personal. The United States Constitution says in Article 4 Section 4 that it is the government's duty to protect its citizens from invasion. The government is not doing this." When she said that, the audience erupted with applause in an uproar of agreement to her statement. Emboldened by the applause, Trudy continued, "We are faced with aliens who are relentless in their push to enter the United States, and those of us who live close to the border have been generous, and, out of kindness, we have fed and given water to countless aliens; we pay our taxes, and in return we are murdered and kidnapped!" At that statement the room exploded a second time with cheers and clapping from the crowd who seemed to be in total agreement with what she had said.

Trudy spoke for several more minutes repeating the same theme and getting several rounds of enthusiastic applause. Next, Raquel introduced Trudy's son, David

Hess, who said, "Most ranchers who live close to the border have been abused in some way or another by outlaw aliens. When I was a kid we always helped people coming through. We gave them water and food, but now we don't help them any longer because we don't want to get into trouble. We see Mexicans with drugs and guns, and we avoid them because we don't want trouble. People who don't live here ask us, 'Why don't you move?' and we answer. We don't move because this is our home. We have a right to be here." At that the crowd broke into cheering and clapping. People rose out of their chairs and clapped.

David talked for another five minutes and then Raquel introduced Larry Herdes, a tall, athletic-looking rancher who lived east of Animas twenty miles. His family had been in the area for a hundred years, living that whole time along the border in the southeast corner of the Bootheel. Larry looked like the movie star Robert Redford, but a little more rugged and masculine. He exuded confidence as he walked to the microphone. "My family has been here a hundred years," Larry said firmly and then he paused letting the longevity of his family's history sink into everyone present. Then he continued, "We have had cattle stolen, and we have been attacked by Mexican federal police who were protecting a marijuana field on the Mexican side of the line. We were minding our own business, working cattle, and were attacked for no reason! People used to sneak across the line to find work, but now they haul drugs. We need the Border Patrol! But we need them on the border!" At this statement a crescendo of applause erupted from the civilians present, whereas the thirty-five or so Border Patrol present sat silent in their chairs looking straight ahead. "We don't need them fifteen or fifty miles north of the border!" And here again another round of applause was interjected.

At last it came time for Jim Yarbrough to be introduced, and Sheila Morris herself came to the podium in place of Raquel. Sheila made the introduction, telling of his fifty years as an Arizona cattleman and experienced speaker about border issues.

Yarbrough stepped up to the podium and took the microphone out of its holder and held it in his right hand. He had no fear in his delivery and sprang forth upon the audience, gesticulating with the hand that did not hold the microphone. He used his finger to point and to make a point. It was obvious that with words he was going to do battle. He looked down at the Border Patrol agent who was the El Paso Sector chief surrounded by his legion of sycophant agents and the bombshell beauty who was his secretary. The sector chief—who was an S.E.S.-level agent, which was a presidential-appointed position, and according to law capable of the same rate of pay as the vice president of the United States or the speaker of the U.S. House of Representatives—and the old cowboy stared each other down. Jim Yarbrough's voice boomed, "We are going to Texas! Down Interstate 10 to Van Horn and then we are going to turn south to Valentine on Highway 90. At no point when you drive from Van Horn through Valentine, Marfa, Alpine and Marathon will you be able to see the Rio Grande River off to your right and miles away. The Rio Grande is the international boundary. Four miles north of Valentine there is a county road that travels twelve miles west to the river. When it reaches the river the road goes downstream sixty miles to the border town of Presidio. In between where it hits the river and reaches Presidio, it travels through the little towns of Candelaria and Ruidosa."

Jim Yarbrough continued his dissertation, "I was down in that county a few months ago, and a cowboy who lives there told me that at sundown the Border Patrol will not go down that road. In other words, there is a sixty-mile stretch of international boundary that the Border Patrol refuses to go to when it's dark outside." The El Paso Sector chief and his companions sat staring at Jim with vengeance in their eyes. He continued, "I asked a rancher friend of mine who owns one of the largest ranches in the area and is also a Presidio County commissioner if the story was true. He told me, yes, and then he said, 'I'll go one farther, the Border Patrol is mad at the county because we maintain that road. They say it just makes it easy on the people hauling drugs and illegal aliens out of the area, and we tell them that we have American citizens down there in Candelaria and Ruidosa, and they need a good road to get to town or for the sheriff or an ambulance to get to them, but the Border Patrol is mad at the county for the maintenance of the road.'"

Jim Yarbrough paused momentarily, letting the significance of his statement sink in. The El Paso Sector chief glared at him while his beautiful secretary took notes. Yarbrough raised his hand to make a point. "On January 7 a cowboy who is a friend of mine was kidnapped south of here about thirty miles in a very remote place. He was abducted twelve miles north of the border. He was taken across state lines into Arizona, which makes it a federal affair. In Lordsburg we have a brand new $20 million Border Patrol station with 200 agents. On any given day 90 percent of the Lordsburg Border Patrol's assets will be deployed north of where my friend was captured. That, ladies and gentlemen, is not an opinion, it is a fact. At this point the crowd clapped with enthusiasm and agreement with what Jim Yarbrough was saying. "The Border Patrol is not on the border!" The uproar coming from the crowd after that statement was the loudest yet; Jim went on as if under the same anointing as Billy Sunday or Billy Graham. "There are lots of good young American men and women in the Border Patrol who are patriots, but they can only do what they are told to do!" The crowd burst forth again with clapping and whistling. "But," Jim Yarbrough said, "if their superior officers tell them to retreat fifty miles north of the border, they must do what they are told!" The El Paso chief glared at Yarbrough who continued. "The Border Patrol is not on the border because politicians in Washington D.C. do not want them there. The politicians in Washington D.C. don't know who or what is coming across the border. We don't need more Border Patrol agents. We don't need a wall. We don't need to appropriate more taxpayers' money. What we need is a warrior and a patriot in the White House!" At this the house came down and everyone stood up except the sector chief and his beautiful companion. The clapping lasted for a good while, and Jim Yarbrough walked back to his chair and sat down next to the other speakers.

Raquel Nunez walked to the podium to speak, but Sheila Morris beat her to the microphone and grabbed it. After glancing at Jim Yarbrough, she looked at the crowd and said rather sarcastically, "Well, we don't have any doubt where he stands, do we?" No one said anything, and she went on, "The New Mexico Cattle Growers' Association does not necessarily endorse anything that is said here this evening. And now I will introduce our next and final speaker this evening. We are fortunate to have the honorable Earnest Dolittle, our congressman from New Mexico's 2nd Congressional District with us tonight. Please welcome Mr. Dolittle as he makes his way to the podium." With that introduction, a scattered offering of applause came forth from the gallery.

Congressman Dolittle, a Republican rumored to have his eye on the governor's mansion, grasped the microphone and held it to his chest and looked out at his audience and took a deep breath accentuating his profound sincerity even before he opened his mouth to speak. "I am embarrassed that our government considers you expendable!" He paused to let those words sink in. "There is some deep rooted belief in Washington that securing the border is not moral. I question the policy of putting the Border Patrol sixty miles north of the border on Highway 9 or Interstate 10. I am embarrassed that our government thinks a wolf or a lizard or a spotted owl is more important than your children! I burn with shame with a government that treats its people that way!" He paused and gave the audience time to clap, and they took the hint and responded. "I challenge anyone who says the border is secure to come and walk the border with me!" No one could remember him ever being on the international boundary on the south side of the Bootheel. "When people come and walk with me they always bring machine guns to keep them safe." He paused for a moment. "Yet we have people in Washington saying the border is secure." He paused again. "I am embarrassed that citizens of the United States can't keep from being stolen from by outlaws south of the border, but the government won't protect you! You can't expect politicians to do the right thing! You have to stay after them." He breathed deeply. "I am embarrassed that the FBI will turn the victim into the perpetrator, and I hear that tonight in the circumstances of this story. So understand, we will bring the FBI state director into this case to investigate. I am incensed when I hear how arrogant agents are twisting stuff around! "

"Don't think people are powerless. The most powerful thing you can do is to speak out. Don't be silent. Make your cry be heard in the streets. It is at that point that the country's moral indignation will rise up and the people in Washington can be changed. So join with me and make your voices be heard across the land."

"God bless you and God bless America."

The crowd rose to its feet, and a crescendo of applause and cheering sprang forth. El Paso's sector chief and his beautiful secretary rose to their feet and clapped, as well as the entourage of green uniforms that surrounded them.

Raquel Nunez went to the podium and thanked everyone for coming and officially ended the meeting. The crowd did not disperse quickly because everyone seemed electrified by the excitement, or perhaps it was the issue at hand. There was a right-wing extremist militia group set up at a table toward the back of the building, and they were passing out literature about their agenda and were asking people to sign various petitions or membership applications. They were also taking donations. The executive committee of the Arizona Cattle Growers' Association was seated at another table discussing their official statement concerning border security. People mingled and talked and shared a thousand horror stories about life on the border.

Way in the back of the building with his back against the wall and one leg lifted so his cowboy boot heel could rest knee high against the cement block wall that was painted white stood Buster Saunders, the county sheriff. He had deliberately stayed back in the shadows all evening, and almost no one had seen him. A cowboy who was employed and rode for the large Las Animas Ranch spied the sheriff who was trying to be incognito. The cowboy approached the sheriff and spoke to him, "So what do you think about all of these Border Patrol agents and politicians, Buster?"

The sheriff thought about the question for a moment and then replied, "I get about $500,000 a year from those people, so I ain't saying anything."

Chapter Sixteen
February 4, 2016

A week after the big town hall meeting at the Animas school auditorium, Ben received a call from the New Mexico State Police asking him if he would be willing to meet with officers from several agencies including the U.S. Border Patrol, the FBI, and the state police. "We just want to clear a few things up - ask a few questions," the officer said. Ben had become very disillusioned with all of the investigators and came close to saying, no, to the officer's request; but, after thinking for a moment, he said, yes, that he would come. He had no feelings of guilt or the need to hide anything, so he wasn't afraid; but on the other hand, he was getting sick of talking to them. And the fact that nothing was ever resolved. He was told that they wanted to meet him at the Lordsburg Border Patrol Station at 10:00 a.m. Thursday, February 4.

Ben left his house early, at 8:00 a.m., with plans on stopping at the Valley Mercantile store in Animas to buy some supplies he needed to help in his work. The Valley Mercantile was a business with everything a rancher or contractor might need. They sold lumber, metal products, plumbing supplies, electrical supplies, feed, tools, nuts and bolts, and fuel, plus groceries, and just about everything else. It was also a convenient gathering place for local residents. There was no café or saloon in town that was open on a steady schedule, so people just naturally ran onto each other at the "Merc."

On his way out the door holding a new grease gun and several tubes of grease he had purchased, Ben ran onto Fred Benson, a local cattle rancher who had lived in the area his entire life. Fred had also been the Hidalgo County sheriff for several terms, as well as a deputy. His terms as acting sheriff had been marked with success in hunting down criminals and keeping the peace. He enjoyed the reputation of having been a good sheriff, even though his last term had ended twenty years earlier, and as a no-nonsense but fair man. He was quiet, the kind of man who held his cards close to his chest where no one could see them. Ben Moody and Fred Benson leaned up against Ben's pickup to visit.

"So, how you doing, Ben?" Fred asked.

"Oh, I guess I'm fine. I'm getting tired of all the bullshit. I wish they would just leave me alone."

"Who's messing with you?"

"Well, I'm headed to Lordsburg right now for my third or fourth meeting with the FBI, the state police, and the Border Patrol. It's the same stupid stuff all of the time, and nothing ever gets resolved. They keep twisting things around and trying to get me to change my story. I'm sick of it."

Fred Benson looked at the ground for a moment as if he was thinking. "Have they ever read you your Miranda rights or advised you to seek the advice of an attorney? Do you have an attorney?"

"No."

Fred paused, thinking. "Listen, you don't have to tell them anything if you don't want to. If they haven't formally charged you with anything, and if they haven't read you your rights or advised you to get an attorney, you are not obligated to answer any questions. You need to take care of yourself. Watch what you say!"

"Thanks," Ben said.

They shook hands and Fred walked toward the door going into the Valley Mercantile. After walking a few feet, he turned and looked at Ben as he was stepping into his pickup. "You've got some friends around here, you know."

"Thanks," Ben answered.

Ben drove north to Lordsburg thirty miles distance and pulled into the Border Patrol's new $20 million station. He walked into the main entrance and was met by one of the same state policeman he had seen at the other meetings, although he had never talked much to the man. "Follow me, Mr. Moody; we just want to ask you a few questions." They went down a hallway and turned left into a room, and Ben heard the state patrolman lock the door of the room after they had walked through it. There, seated in a chair, was Celia, She stood and introduced him to another woman who stood and offered her hand. "This is Amanda Woodruff from our Albuquerque office. She is going to ask you a few questions."

"I want my personal belongings back," Ben said, looking at Celia. "It's my understanding you found my pistol and my cell phone. I want you to give them back to me."

"We ran a check on your firearm, talking to Jorganson's gun store in Willcox, to make sure you purchased it legally. All of that checked out fine, everything was handled according to law, so we turned your firearm over to the New Mexico State Police, and they are holding it at this time," Celia said.

Ben looked at the state trooper who had met him at the door and led him down the hallway and then locked the door behind him. "I want my pistol back," Ben said.

"I'm not sure where your gun is, Mr. Moody. I will look into that," the man said.

"I want my cell phone back. You've got that too."

"We had to get into your phone, Mr. Moody. And after getting the information we wanted, we dipped it in acid. I'm afraid your phone is no longer able to function," Celia said.

A sound came from the door of the room as someone using a key unlocked it, and two men in green uniforms walked in. One of the men was Patrol Agent in Charge Clair Ainsley, who had questioned Ben at the Animas Community Center during his first interrogation the day he returned from Willcox. The other agent was introduced as James Bobbitt, an internal investigator of the agency.

"We need some more information, Mr. Moody," the patrol agent in charge said. "Would you be willing to take a lie detector test?"

"Nothing was said about a lie detector test," Ben said.

"Surely," Celia interjected, "you don't have a problem with a lie detector test. It's just a formality. You don't have anything to hide, do you?"

"No, I don't have anything to hide," Ben said.

"Let's move into another room," Celia said, and they led Ben into an adjacent room and shut the door. As if well acquainted with the drill, all of the people in the room put their signatures on a legal looking piece of paper. Ben supposed that they were signing the official witness statement concerning the test he was about to take. When they had all put their signatures on the paper, they walked out of the room shutting the door, leaving Ben and FBI agent Amanda Woodruff who was going to give Ben the test. She asked Ben to sit down on the opposite side of a table from her. She had a computer in front of her which she busied herself turning on.

"I need you to sign this affidavit, "Agent Woodruff told Ben.

"Sign what? I don't see anything to sign."

"Here on the computer, use this stylus and sign your name there on that line." Agent Woodruff pointed to a line on the screen.

"I'm not signing anything."

"It's just saying you have agreed to take the test."

"I'm not going to put my signature on something I don't understand."

"Here," she pointed with her finger at some writing on the computer's screen. "You can read it."

Ben looked at it, and the font was very small, and his eyes couldn't adjust well enough to read it. "I can't read it."

"Okay, I'll read it to you," and she took off reading several paragraphs of legal jargon that Ben had no understanding of. He doubted if Amanda Woodruff understood it. He took the stylus and scribbled something that looked Chinese, or less understandable. It was nothing like his official signature, but in spite of that, Amanda Woodruff seemed pleased.

Amanda asked Ben to sit back and relax in his chair and let her attach several small electric sensors to Ben's head, these having small rubber suction cup tips that were supposed to lay flat against his skin but there was suction taking place, so she taped them in place with medical tape. Then she wrapped his chest with a cloth strap having electrical looking wires coming out of the ends of the strap. All of these wires from the electrodes on his skull and the strap around his chest were plugged into a control box of some kind that was then connected into Amanda's computer. Ben almost laughed while all of this hooking up took place but then put on his straightest face when the female FBI agent sat down in her chair and asked him, "Okay are you ready to go through with this?"

"Sure," Ben said. "Go for it."

"How many lights do you see in this room?" Amanda questioned.

Ben looked around, counting electric lights that were glowing but then realized that there were several that were turned off. "Do you mean all of the lights or just the ones that are turned on?"

"Just the ones that are turned on."

"Thirteen."

When Ben answered, Amanda moved her mouse around doing something with the computer, but the screen was facing away from Ben so he couldn't see what she was doing. She also did some typing on the computer keyboard.

"Have you ever stolen anything from your employer?"

"No." Ben replied and then more movement came from the agent's hands doing something with her computer.

"How many miles is it from Willcox to Animas?"

"About eighty, I suppose."

"How long have you known the men that you helped haul the drugs from the border to Interstate 10?"

"I didn't help anyone haul drugs anywhere!"

"Answer the question please, Mr. Moody. How long have you known them?"

"I never met or saw any of them before January 7," Ben said.

"How many men did you meet on January 7?" the FBI agent asked.

"I didn't meet any of them. I don't know how many there were."

"Is it true there were only five of them?" she asked.

"I don't know how many there were, but I'm sure there were more than five. Probably ten or twelve," Ben replied.

"Then you counted them?" the agent asked.

"No, I did not count them."

"How much money did they pay you to help them get the drugs through Animas and on to the interstate?"

"They didn't pay me any money!" *This lady is a bitch,* Ben thought to himself.

During this whole process Amanda had been typing and maneuvering her mouse around the mouse pad. "That's pretty good," she said. "But that was just a trial run, now we will do it again. I've got the computer program working correctly."

They went through the same questions again and Ben gave the same answers, and Amanda the FBI agent worked diligently with her mouse and the keys on the computer keyboard. Ben had no idea what she was doing. After a considerable amount of computer manipulating she looked at Ben and announced, "You are screwed!"

"Excuse me?" Ben said.

"You are screwed? Big time! You are guilty as hell!"

"How do you figure?" Ben began pulling suction cups and straps off his body.

"You are going to prison. You are lying like hell, cowboy!" The FBI agent said as she turned the computer screen around so Ben could see it. "See the results? Right here—read it yourself." She pointed to a spot on the screen that read 98 percent negative. "That means you failed the test. You have a failure rate of 98 percent. You are a habitual liar."

Ben stood up, and without replying to Amanda, whom he was now convinced was exceedingly wicked if not downright crazy, he walked to the door that had originally let him into the room. Walking through that door put Ben back into the room he had been led into by the New Mexico state trooper, and sitting there waiting for him was Celia, the patrol agent in charge of the Lordsburg Station, the Border Patrol investigator, and the state trooper. "Well I don't know what else I can tell you people. I really don't have anything to say. This lady just gave me a lie detector test and said I was 98 percent wrong; in other words, I'm lying all of the time. She said I was screwed. That's the word she used: screwed. She said I was going to prison. I haven't even been charged with anything." Ben remained standing, looking at the locked door.

"We need you to sign this paper admitting that you are lying or we are going to arrest you," Celia said.

Ben stared at them one by one, beginning with Celia and then going to the state trooper, the patrol agent in charge, and then the Border Patrol investigator. "You haven't told me what my rights are. You haven't advised me to get myself an attorney, and you haven't officially charged me with anything. I'm not going to sign anything!"

"You're lying." Amanda had sat down behind him after following him back into this room. Ben turned and looked at her when she spoke.

"I now have a record of you lying. You know you lie! If you want us to think you are innocent we are going to need more information." Ben turned and faced Celia as she said that. "We know that you have been down to the border again," the Border Patrol investigator said. "We have been tracking you."

"How are you tracking me?" Ben asked.

"We have phone records," Celie answered.

Ben had purchased a new cell phone several weeks before to replace the one the FBI and state police wouldn't give back to him. For four or five days the phone had been sounding funny, as if he was talking down into a long, hollow pipe. When talking to someone, the phone would make crackling sounds, and he could hear noises in the background. It reminded him of the old rural party-lines that people had when he was a kid. He knew that they were listening to his conversations. "Is it against the law for me to go down toward the border?" he asked.

"What are you doing down there?" Celia asked.

"None of your damn business what I'm doing down there," Ben said.

"Look here mister smarty pants, don't get rude with me. I can arrest you!" Celia snapped.

"For what? Doing my job?"

"She's asking you a legitimate question, Mr. Moody. Tell us what you've got on the border," the Lordsburg patrol agent in charge said, trying to act civil.

"Sometimes I work down there. I've got witnesses. If you were doing your job you would be down there also, but I've never seen you there. Why not?"

"You're walking on thin ice, Mr. Moody. Don't get too smart," Celia warned him and then went on. "There are inconsistencies in your story. Things don't add up."

"Like what?"

"For instance, why did you unload 1,500 pounds of good marijuana out in a cow pasture eight miles north of Animas?" Celia queried.

"I didn't unload 1,500 pounds of dope north of Animas. An outlaw Mexican did, and he had a pistol, and he told me I better get to helping him, so I did! My hands were tied. Did you ever try to wrestle an armed outlaw with your hands tied together?"

"Your fingerprints were on that marijuana. We know you helped unload it. Why were you so cooperative?" Celia questioned.

Ben stared at her in unbelief. She went on, "That brings up another inconsistency in your story, another little thing that makes you look guilty as hell. It's the little things that a professional notices in a habitual liar's testimony."

"What are you talking about?" Ben interrupted her.

"Small things that don't make any sense. For instance, in our first interview I questioned you about how you answered a call of nature; and you told me that the guard, whom you claim was watching you, allowed you to stand up and unzip your pants and relieve yourself. Your hands were tied in front of you, and the guard did not untie your hands. That's impossible, Mr. Moody. You're not telling the whole story." Celia was becoming angry.

"What do you mean, it's impossible? I stood up with my hands tied and unzipped my pants and took a leak. That's not impossible."

"Maybe that's possible, Mr. Moody, but you haven't told us the whole story!" Celia was now almost screaming.

"What in the world are you talking about?" Ben asked quietly.

"Mr. Moody, you cannot poop and clean yourself with your hands tied in front of you. Explain that to us, Mr. Moody." Celia was gritting her teeth.

"I didn't poop."

"Didn't poop!" Celia rose out of her chair and slammed a notebook that she had carried into the room down on the table so hard the table bounced up off of the tile floor. She screamed, "Mr. Moody, everyone in those situations has to poop. That is the kind of evidence we professionals listen for because we know that everyone in stressful situations always needs to poop. If you are innocent, you would have needed to poop, and you insist that you didn't need to."

"I didn't need to."

"For twenty-four hours? You are a liar!" Celia grabbed her notebook and threw it across the room where it crashed into a wall twenty feet away. "You are a liar!" She screamed and stomped over and picked up her notebook and papers that were cast about the floor.

"You are not cooperating, Mr. Moody," The state patrolman said while Celia marched back across toward Ben and slammed her notebook back down on the table, glaring at him as she did so.

"Look," Ben said, "I understand that maybe you guys aren't telling me everything. I understand that there could be some things that you can't tell me. I have thought that maybe you had an undercover agent out there that day, and you're trying to protect him. Maybe that's why you watched me at the truck stop in Willcox and didn't try to help me. Maybe you've got somebody that's in trouble and you are trying to protect them. I'm alright with that. If that's what's going on, I'm alright with that. Maybe something else is going on here that you are trying to hide. But I don't care anymore. I'm done! I haven't done anything wrong, and I'm not a criminal, and I'm leaving here, and I'm not going to talk to you again."

"What a total bunch of bullshit!" Celia screamed, and she swooped up her paperwork in one fluid motion with her arms and headed toward the locked door. "Let me out of here!" she ordered the state trooper who almost tripped over himself scrambling to open the door before she berated him or perhaps slapped him, which is what he feared. "It is completely impossible to get anything done when you're surrounded by idiots," Celia muttered as she walked out the door and stomped down the hall toward some cubicle of misery where she hoped to collect herself.

Ben Moody started walking toward the doorway that had just been unlocked for Celia. "Here, Mr. Moody," the patrol agent in charge said while stepping out in front of Ben and reaching into his pocket and retrieving a business card which he offered to Ben, "Please take this and give me a call in case you ever have anything I can help you with."

Like the patrol agent in charge, the state trooper and Border Patrol investigator offered Ben their business cards, repeating their coworkers words, "Yes, please, Mr. Moody, give us a call if there is anything we can do for you."

Ben took their cards but walked away in utter amazement. One minute they were calling him a liar and bragging about arresting him, and the next minute they were begging him to take their business cards as if they were all car salesmen. He walked away determined to not have any more to do with them, business cards or no business cards.

When Ben reached his pickup, he called his father on his cell phone to give him a report on the meeting with law enforcement that he had just left. Just as it had been doing for several days, the sound coming from his phone made hollow clicking sounds, and he thought that he was probably being listened to by some FBI agent. He told his father about his suspicions about his phone being bugged.

Ben's father had been a high-level supervisor for one of the largest construction companies in the world and had spent several years working on a stretch of wall the United States government had built on the Mexican border near Nogales, Arizona. While on that job, one of the men who worked for Ben's father had been falsely accused of smuggling contraband across the international boundary. FBI and U. S. Customs officials really went after the guy in an attempt to arrest him but were unable to because of a lack of evidence. In the process of their attempt to arrest the guy, which lasted for a month or more, they bugged his phone and started listening to all of his conversations. The phone was provided to the man by the construction company that he and Ben's father worked for. The phone made weird noises exactly like Ben's phone was doing.

After several weeks, the man and Ben's father figured out what was happening, and they mentioned it to members of the upper-level management of the huge construction company who, in turn, instructed the company's attorneys to put a stop to the phone tapping. The construction company's attorneys were members of one of California's most prestigious law firms based in Los Angeles. The Los Angeles attorneys knew the correct buttons to push, and the noises and odd sounds on the man's cell phone stopped because the wiretapping stopped.

Ben's father related this story to his son after Ben gave his dad a report about his meeting with Celia and the others that he had just left at the Lordsburg Border Patrol Station. "If they don't quit listening to your phone conversations I will make a call to those attorneys in Los Angeles." He mentioned the law firm by name. The hollow clicking noises coming out of Ben's phone stopped immediately at the mention of the law firm in Los Angeles, and Ben never heard anything out of the ordinary on his phone again.

Chapter Seventeen
February 15, 2016

In private conversation, Congressman Dolittle promised his constituents in Hidalgo County that he would press hard on the powers-that-be in the nation's capital to improve security on the Mexican border. He said that he would put extra effort into working with the House of Representatives' Homeland Security committee to insure that increased funding would be made available to furnish the Border Patrol with more radar units, helicopters, electronic ground sensors, and more agents. It was suggested by several residents that the government should finance the building of more cell phone towers south of Highway 9 so residents in the remote faraway places in the Bootheel could have cell service in case of emergency. The congressman promised the people he would look into that. Lots of ideas were discussed and promises made. Everyone who had attended the town hall meeting at Animas had heard the famous congressman say that he was ashamed of his country who thought Bootheel residents were "expendable."

Everyone had heard him say that he was unhappy that the FBI and other agencies had twisted the story around making the victim (Ben Moody) look like a perpetrator. That was the word he had used in his speech at the Animas school auditorium and people remembered it. The New

Mexico Cattle Growers' Association had a professional photographer film the meeting, and the congressman's speech was recorded and put on the internet.

To prove his sincerity about border security being a serious matter as well as to create good will among Bootheel residents, the good congressman arranged for Betty Davis to come and testify to congress in front of the House Committee on Homeland Security. With the help of the congresswoman representing Arizona's 2nd Congressional District, who had campaigned and won with emphasis on border security, it was arranged that another woman, Mavis Alexander, would testify at the same time. Mrs. Alexander was the wife of a well-known cattle rancher, Jim Alexander, whose ranch lay in Santa Cruz County, south of Tucson and west of Nogales. The Alexanders had suffered much because of Narco traffic, and both Mr. and Mrs. Alexander had been very vocal in their opinions. They had been to many meetings with top Border Patrol brass, as well as numerous senators and congressmen. They had been quoted in newspapers and had appeared on television many times. Mrs. Alexander was eighty years old, weighed 95 pounds soaking wet, and was afraid of nobody including the president of the United States, or Mexico for that matter. She was going to show up in Washington prepared and ready to do battle.

The two ladies did not know each other prior to their trip to the nation's capital but met at the airport in Tucson and traveled together. They hit it off immediately, and when the airplane touched down at Reagan International, they were excited. Sitting on the plane waiting for their turn to disembark, they looked out of the window and across the Potomac River and saw the Washington Monument rising like a beacon to truth and honesty where it stood in the middle of the National Mall only several miles away.

They stayed together, enjoying each other's company, and engaged a taxi to drive them to the Phoenix Park Hotel, which was only three blocks north of the capital building. The cab driver was an immigrant from Lebanon whose English was hard to understand because of his Middle Eastern accent but his efficiency as a cab driver was supercharged by his uncanny ability to dart in and out and across multiple lanes of traffic at speeds that were obviously above the law. His quickness of eye and explanations of points of interest they were speeding by made the ride from Reagan International to the Phoenix Park Hotel feel like they were in a foreign country. It was exciting. He sped up to the main entry of the hotel, which had a red cloth awning reaching out onto the sidewalk, and a doorman dressed in an ornate uniform walked up and opened the taxi door and assisted Mrs. Alexander's exit from the taxi. The Lebanese taxi driver opened the door for Betty Davis and then busied himself extracting their luggage from the trunk of the car.

The Phoenix Park Hotel did not have the largest or most beautiful lobby one could ever see, but its appointments were nice, with enough dark mahogany wood to make it look expensive in an old colonial way. Its location near the epicenter of the world's greatest country's very core of decision making was exhilarating.

After getting settled into their rooms, Betty Davis and Mavis Alexander met at the Dubliner Pub and Restaurant located on the ground level of the hotel. The Dubliner claimed the distinction of selling more Guinness than any other establishment on the North American continent, as well as serving very fine food. It was packed with a mob of humanity eating and drinking. The men, for the most part, were wearing ties that had been loosened for relief after a hard day's work at the office. The female patrons of the Dubliner were dressed in smart-looking business suits and dresses, wearing expensive-looking shoes. Everyone was talking loudly with a spirit of exuberance and lust for mixing with people who were in the know about everything pertaining to what was important in the most important city. Betty and Mavis thought the loud and rowdy place must surely be filled with staffers from senators' and congressmen's offices, as well as assistants to foreign dignitaries and perhaps a spy or two. Eager to try the pub's famous food, Betty ordered Guinness braised beef, and Mavis asked for Irish beef stew. While dining they discussed the speeches they had prepared for their meeting the next day with the House of Representatives' Committee on Homeland Security. But mostly they marveled at the loud crowd, all of whom seemed to be engaged in excited and urgent conversation while drinking copious amounts of Guinness or hard liquor.

In the morning the two ladies asked the doorman to hail them a cab for the short ride to the capital where a staffer from Congressman Dolittle's office met them at the door to the House of Representatives' annex and led them inside. Soon a member of the congresswoman from Arizona's 2nd Congressional District's office led Mavis Alexander to her office, and Betty Davis was taken to Congressman Dolittle's office. Both of these members of the house were very busy, so after a very short courtesy call, the staffers showed them the way to a gallery where the House Committee on Homeland Security was about to meet. The staffers, one from Arizona and the other from New Mexico, introduced the ladies to a secretary who asked to see the manuscripts of their prepared speeches; and so they gave them to her. The secretary said she would bring them back shortly and walked away. Another secretary offered the ladies, who by this time had become fast friends, a place to sit down, which they did. After ten minutes the first secretary returned with the prepared manuscripts that had been handed to her. They looked at them and immediately saw that certain parts of their speeches had been blocked out and made unreadable by using a felt-tipped pen. They were politely instructed to read only the words that were left on the page.

This development took the women by surprise, but before they were able to discuss how they would deal with the new instructions they were led into the gallery where the committee meeting was about to convene. The congresswoman from Arizona was a member of the committee so she was going to be part of the meeting, but Congressman Dolittle was not on that committee, so he was not present.

The meeting moved fast, and in between trying to follow what was taking place and studying their newly edited manuscripts, Betty and Mavis suddenly felt unprepared. It was soon obvious to both of them that they were not the stars of the show like they had been made to believe. They had been told that they could tell the truth about the lack of security on the Mexican border, but with their edited manuscripts, they felt the message was watered down.

Betty was asked to testify first and responded by reading what was left of her speech. She was asked several questions by members of the committee and then her turn was over. There were several other people besides Betty and Mavis who needed a turn to speak. Mavis was next, and she threw caution and her manuscript to the wind. She obviously had decided that no constraints were going to be put on her freedom of speech, and the opportunity to address politicians who drew wages derived from her tax money. She let them have the version that had not been watered down. Members of the committee sat looking at her over the rims of their glasses that were positioned out on the ends of their noses. Surprisingly she was able to get a considerable amount of her unvarnished narrative out before the chairman of the committee proceeded to shut her down. They have ways of dealing with runaway speeches and speakers, even if they are elderly women. Her microphone was shut off.

Mavis was no dummy. They had stifled her message and she had fought back. She was not embarrassed, ashamed, or sorry; and so the meeting went on, and when it was over, the two women were treated with respect and then led down the hallways to the respective offices of their congressman and congresswoman.

Betty Davis entered Congressman Earnest Dolittle's office and found him behind his desk typing on the keyboard of his computer. The congressman looked up and saw his constituent from the far southwest corner of this congressional district and he stood up and said, "Well, how did the meeting go? Did my partners in crime treat you well?" He smiled broadly, proud of his witty comment.

"It was fine, I guess, but not exactly what I was expecting," Betty answered.

"How so?"

"To begin with, they edited both Mavis' and my speeches that we had prepared, and, at least in my case, it ruined my train of thought, so I really doubt that I said anything of value. Mavis Alexander, she went ahead and said what she wanted. She didn't pay any attention to her edited script, and I think they turned her microphone off. They cut her off and silenced her, but she got several licks in before that. Told them that the United States government and the Department of Homeland Security had no Idea who or what was coming across the border. That was the main part of her manuscript they had crossed out, but she told them anyway. They asked me several questions, mainly out of politeness I think, but they didn't ask her any questions. It was obvious they wanted her out of there, so they moved on to the next speaker and ignored her. Why did they do that?"

"You have to understand that these people here have a busy schedule, and they are only going to deal with the issues that they want to. Usually what they want to deal with depends on which side of the isle they sit on, and so the questions they field and the answers they give may or may not be the questions and answers that you were hoping for. They are not, at least in their opinions, obligated to entertain any guest, or question of any guest, or opinion of any guest. They gave you as much attention as they felt like you deserved," Mr. Dolittle said.

"But," Betty Davis said, "that's not fair, I'm a taxpayer! This is supposed to be a government of the people, for the people, and by the people!"

Congressman Dolittle chuckled a little and then paused for a second before he continued, "They don't care about people very much, at least not as much as they care about their own agendas. They are busy, and they don't think you have all of the facts. For the most part, their minds are made up one way or the other anyway."

"Why then did we bother coming out here?" she asked.

"I was hoping it would go better for you, but sometimes these meetings are like this."

"When you were in Animas you promised that you would have the FBI's main man in New Mexico look into why Ben Moody has been accused of working with the

Mexican drug cartels. You said that you were ashamed of the way our country had treated him. Have you spoken to anyone about that problem?"

"No, I haven't gotten around to that, but, in reality, I wasn't convinced of his story. It's very hard to confront the FBI if you're not sure that something really happened that they need to deal with."

Now Betty was mad, and she said, "Well, something damn sure happened!"

"Actually," he said, "I think he's guilty as hell!"

Chapter Eighteen
May 6, 2016
Sunup

Highway 9 begins, at its western end, where it leaves U.S. Highway 80 about six miles north of Rodeo, New Mexico; and it then goes straight east fourteen miles to Animas, and then on to Hatchita, Columbus, and eventually Santa Teresa, which is a short distance west of El Paso. Between Highway 80 and Animas, Highway 9 goes over a mountain pass known locally as Antelope Pass. The mountains that Antelope Pass dissect are the Peloncillos, which are really nothing more than a long line of rocky hills and canyons that go south in close proximity to the Arizona/New Mexico border and eventually becomes part of the great Sierra Madre. The Peloncillos are not high in altitude, but, nevertheless, they are very wild and remote. They are inhabited by mountain lions and an occasional jaguar coming up out of Mexico, as well as big horn sheep, several species of deer, coati bears, black bears, and numerous species of rattlesnakes, several of which are on the endangered species list. The Peloncillos are also the safest route for alien traffic to use anywhere between the Gulf of Mexico to the Pacific Ocean. The Border Patrol, except on very rare occasions, do not venture into this narrow strip of rocky crags and canyons, but, instead, they lay in wait in the San Simon

Valley, on the Arizona side of the mountain range, or the Animas Valley, on the New Mexico side; or they closely watch Highway 9 and Antelope Pass, which is a full forty miles north of the international boundary.

May 6 was a Friday, and at 7 a.m. eight illegal aliens descended down the northern slope of Gray Mountain, one of the many peaks in the Peloncillo range, and proceeded to cross Highway 9 about one mile west of the top of the shallow pass. The group was made up of five men from Guatemala, two from the Mexican state of Chiapas, and one man, who was the group's guide and leader, hailed from Janos Chihuahua, a mere seventy-five miles to the southeast.

The crossing of the highway, at this time, was no coincidence but was in fact a well-planned strategic move. The men from Guatemala and Chiapas were carrying small fifteen-pound packs of low-quality marijuana, plus some extra underwear, socks, and a toothbrush. The Mexican from Janos was carrying a pack with a few cans of Vienna sausages, refried beans, and Jumex juice, as well as some socks and a toothbrush. More importantly he had a cell phone, and when he and his companions reached a spot 500 yards from the highway they stopped at the Janos man's command and waited while he held his cell phone in his hand. At a quarter past seven, he received a call from an individual who was sitting six miles to the west in a parked car at the intersection of Highway 80 and Highway 9. When a Border Patrol agent coming from Lordsburg and traveling south on 80 reached this intersection and turned left, driving east on Highway 9, the individual sitting in the parked car called the man from Janos and informed him of the Border Patrol agent who was now headed his way. The man in the parked car calculated the distance and told the man from Janos that the Border Patrol agent would be near his position in seven or eight minutes.

After receiving this call, the man from Janos told the seven men with the fifteen-pound packs of marijuana that the coast was clear, "Vamanos. Caminar de esa," the Janos man said pointing toward the highway and the country on the highway's other side, which was off in a northerly direction. As the men packing the drugs walked toward the highway the man from Janos slyly dropped back, walking at a much slower pace, "No te detengas en la carretera! Ve al otro lado." Don't stop at the road. Keep going to the other side, the Janos man said in Spanish, and then, without the other men realizing what was happening, he disappeared, turning off to the side; and then retreating upward through rocks and brush, he vanished. The timing was perfect. The men from Guatemala and Chiapas were in the middle of the pavement when the Border Patrol agent rounded a bend in the road, and there they were, a hundred yards distance.

"Alto! Alto!" the Border Patrol agent hollered as he jumped out of his white and green pickup. The seven aliens had never been in the United States before. They did not know the drill. They didn't have the sense to run. They only looked around for the scout, the man from Janos, thinking he could muster up a solution to their predicament; but to their surprise he had vanished. By the time the seven aliens had come to their wits, it was too late to run because the federal agent in the green uniform was upon them ordering them to put their packs down and their hands up. They were clueless to the fact that they were now looking at several years in a penitentiary in the U.S. for possessing fifteen pounds of dope that a true connoisseur of weed would have thrown out. They had been used.

At the same time and nineteen miles to the south-southwest as a crow flies or eleven miles south of Rodeo near the Geronimo Surrenders Monument on Highway 80, eight veteran Narcos, all from the Sierra Madre west of Casas Grandes, Chihuahua, lay in wait among the desert willows and mesquites that grew along Jackwood Creek. They hid among the trees downstream 200 yards from the bridge that spanned the creek bed which most of the time was nothing more than a dry sand wash. These men, all of whom were dressed in camouflaged military fatigues, were each packing twenty-five pounds of cocaine. The cocaine the men were packing had a street value of $25,000 per pound in Denver, and so each man was carrying $625,000 of cartel assets.

The attempted crossing of Highway 9 by los pobres from Chiapas and Guatemala was a part of the same operation as the eight men lying in wait among the mesquites and willows on Jackwood Creek. The marijuana the pobres were carrying was of little value, and as far as the cartel was concerned, the men from Chiapas and Guatemala were nothing but expendable hardware. They had given the cartel $2000 apiece for safe passage to Interstate 10 where the cartel had told them they could easily catch a ride on north to somewhere like Phoenix or Los Angeles. For $2000 the cartel had also given the men the privilege to pack drugs for them. They had been told, "If you won't pack drugs for us, we won't take you to I-10." They had not been told that they would become human decoys deliberately placed at a strategic spot that would occupy several Border Patrol agents for an hour or more.

The attempted crossing over Highway 9 had taken place during a Border Patrol shift change, which meant there would not be as many agents to arrest and process

los pobres, and so any available agents that would have been deployed south on Highway 80 from the Lordsburg Station were immediately sent to assist the agent who had successfully stopped the four men from Guatemala and the two from Chiapas. The fact that the men were packing drugs made it even more important. And so between 7:00 a.m. and 9:00 a.m. that morning there were no agents from Lordsburg south of the intersection of Highway 9 and U.S. Highway 80.

Agents coming north on U.S. Highway 80 from the Douglas Border Patrol Station were another matter. The cartel had operatives coming north from the town of Douglas. Two cars, both driven by residents of Douglas, one a female the age of twenty-two driving a white Honda Civic and the other a male the age of twenty-five and the boyfriend of the girl in the Honda Civic, drove north on 80 leaving Douglas at 7:00 a.m. The man, driving a Ford pickup, and the girl stopped twelve miles north of town in front of the old Silver Creek Steakhouse and visited for a minute. Then the man left in his Ford pickup and drove north. Ten minutes later the girl followed. They both drove the speed limit or, perhaps, even five miles an hour slower. They broke no laws with the exception of talking on their cell phones, but they had them on speaker phone and no one knew what they were doing.

As they drove along they took note of the location of any Border Patrol or other law enforcement vehicles they saw. At 7:50 a.m. the man in the Ford pickup drove past the Geronimo Monument, and a few seconds later he crossed over the Jackwood bridge. He had no idea there were eight men from Chihuahua hiding in the shadows a hundred yards east of the bridge. He had only been told to seek and find the position of law enforcement between the Apache school, a half mile south of the

los pobres, and so any available agents that would have been deployed south on Highway 80 from the Lordsburg Station were immediately sent to assist the agent who had successfully stopped the four men from Guatemala and the two from Chiapas. The fact that the men were packing drugs made it even more important. And so between 7:00 a.m. and 9:00 a.m. that morning there were no agents from Lordsburg south of the intersection of Highway 9 and U.S. Highway 80.

Agents coming north on U.S. Highway 80 from the Douglas Border Patrol Station were another matter. The cartel had operatives coming north from the town of Douglas. Two cars, both driven by residents of Douglas, one a female the age of twenty-two driving a white Honda Civic and the other a male the age of twenty-five and the boyfriend of the girl in the Honda Civic, drove north on 80 leaving Douglas at 7:00 a.m. The man, driving a Ford pickup, and the girl stopped twelve miles north of town in front of the old Silver Creek Steakhouse and visited for a minute. Then the man left in his Ford pickup and drove north. Ten minutes later the girl followed. They both drove the speed limit or, perhaps, even five miles an hour slower. They broke no laws with the exception of talking on their cell phones, but they had them on speaker phone and no one knew what they were doing.

As they drove along they took note of the location of any Border Patrol or other law enforcement vehicles they saw. At 7:50 a.m. the man in the Ford pickup drove past the Geronimo Monument, and a few seconds later he crossed over the Jackwood bridge. He had no idea there were eight men from Chihuahua hiding in the shadows a hundred yards east of the bridge. He had only been told to seek and find the position of law enforcement between the Apache school, a half mile south of the bridge, and the New Mexico state line, nine miles to the north. The girl in the Honda Civic stopped where the Skeleton Canyon Road left Highway 80, which was where the one-room country school was located. Neither the girl in the Honda nor the man in the Ford pickup had seen a Border Patrol vehicle since passing one at mile marker 402, four miles south of Apache. When the man in the pickup reached the New Mexico state line he told the girl to turn south and drive toward Douglas. When she got to mile marker 402 she saw the Border Patrol agent sitting in his vehicle looking to the south through binoculars. She called her boyfriend and told him what she had seen and then stopped a half mile away and watched the agent.

Among the eight men hiding along Jackwood Creek is our old friend Vidal Garcia Pizarro. In the culture of the lower class Narco laborers who pack heavy fifty-pound bales of marijuana north of the line, most of these human mules never receive much reward or recognition for the dangerous work they do. They are expendable. There are many willing bodies to choose from, like choosing a few good horses or mules out of a corral where there are a hundred or more. If you wear one out or you cripple him, you simply get another. But Vidal Garcia Pizarro is different, and because of that, the other seven are different also. They are thoroughbreds and have been set apart. Vidal is so successful at his vocation that he almost demands his own price. The cocaine packed by this bunch is worth $2,625,000. Vidal's mission was to deliver the cocaine to the Jackwood bridge. His superiors promised to take care of all the other details. Vidal handpicked his crew, hiring men that he had traveled north with on other trips. He made sure they were promised $1500 apiece for the work which would take four days. Usually human mules would get just a couple hundred - maybe. Vidal himself was promised $5000.

Vidal packed no cocaine, only a small pack with a little food and water. He had a F.N. 5.7X28mm pistol with 100 rounds of ammunition. The 5.7X28 is known as the cop killer because of its ability to penetrate the sheet metal found in the average car body and still have enough force left to kill someone after going through a car door. It is semi-automatic and doesn't weigh much. It was given to him by a cartel boss as a gift. Vidal was very much in control.

He and his seven companions had crossed over the international boundary less than a mile from where the corners of Arizona and New Mexico meet the nation of Mexico. They had followed the spine of the Peloncillos going north, crossing the road known as the Geronimo Trail and continuing on crossing the head of Skeleton Canyon and climbing up again until they reached Deer Creek. Here, at the head of Deer Creek Canyon, they stopped and rested until 8:00 p.m. Then they rose up and walked down the Deer Creek drainage, staying in the mesquite and low places as they walked west. They stayed north of the Skeleton Canyon Road, and when they were a mile and a half east of the Apache school, they crawled through the fence and onto the ranch that crazy old Jim Yarbrough took care of. Walking on the other side of an old abandoned farm and what once had been a small feedlot, they kept walking west through mesquite brush and four-winged saltbush until they reached the willows and mesquites along Jackwood Creek. When they got within a half mile of the Jackwood bridge on the highway they stopped and rested. It was 2:00 a.m.

A lot had happened since the fiasco Vidal had been involved with when the cartel sent five truckloads of marijuana north under the leadership of Ray Martinez, the jefe. Vidal had never known the full details of all that had happened on that trip. He had heard that only three of the five loads of dope had made it to their destination. He never knew, for sure, what had become of the poor gringo the jefe had captured, but the rumors were that the man had survived. Vidal had heard that the jefe ran afoul of some police in Denver and had been shot and killed, "Quien sabe. He was a hijo de chingado anyway."

As he sat waiting for sunup Vidal thought about all of these things. He didn't really know the true value in American street dollars of the cocaine he and his companions were delivering, but he knew it was in the millions. He also knew that this was a very professionally run operation with multiple people on the American side helping, making sure it would be a success. He also knew that everyone involved was getting paid better than the usual amount a mule made to carry a load of marijuana north. He was proud of the fact that his reputation and success had enabled him to reach the pinnacle of the smuggling business. At least it was the pinnacle as far as his experience had taught him.

At 7:59 a handsome young man driving a white Toyota Avalon approached the Apache school doing sixty miles an hour in an area where the speed limit was sixty-five. The car did not have tinted windows or anything to attract attention. The handsome young man was well-groomed and wearing no moustache. His hair was neatly trimmed and he wore clean street cloths, the type that an up and coming executive might wear. He was very professional looking. Four and a half miles south of Apache, he passed a girl in a Honda Civic that was parked alongside the highway off of the westbound lane. He knew who and what she was, but she knew nothing about him. A half mile farther he passed a Border Patrol agent looking off to the south through a pair of binoculars. As he had passed the agent he called a number using technology enabling him to talk without holding his phone. The man in the Ford pickup sitting at the New Mexico line twelve miles away answered, "Listo."

The handsome young man now dialed a different number as he slowed down to fifty. "Bueno," Vidal Garcia Pizzaro answered from the other end of the call.

"Dos millas," the handsome young man said. Vidal did not answer. The handsome young man looked into the rear view mirror and saw nobody following. He drove past the Apache school and the intersection of Skeleton Canyon Road and saw nothing. As he crossed the Jackwood bridge he looked forward and backward and saw nothing either direction. Immediately after crossing the bridge he pulled off of the highway and skidded to a stop. Using an electric switch he unlocked the car's trunk as he stepped out and ran to the back of the car where Vidal Garcia Pizzaro and seven other men wearing camouflage fatigues appeared as if out of nowhere to throw seven fifteen-pound tightly and very neatly wrapped packages into the trunk of the car. The handsome young man slammed the trunk shut and quickly got in and was doing sixty miles per hour in about four seconds. The eight men dressed in camouflage disappeared into the creek bed and the willows and mesquites.

The nondescript white Toyota Avalon rolled on north on Highway 80 never exceeding the speed limit. Highway 80 had never had a permanent Border Patrol checkpoint and there had been more illegal drugs hauled up that highway than any other. When the handsome young man reached I-10, he turned east toward Lordsburg, seventeen miles away; and reaching that point, he left I-10 and went north to Silver City. From there he continued north on U.S. Highway 180, which he followed to Reserve, and then he cut through Apache Creek, and Quemado; and at Grants he crossed Interstate 40 and proceeded north to Chama, Alamosa, and finally Denver. His chances of getting stopped and checked by an officer with a drug dog along this route were nonexistent.

Vidal and his companions lay up at the very spot where they had rested from 2:00 a.m. until 6:30 that very morning. As the sun went down, at about the same time Ben and Caroline Moody were sitting down to dinner twenty-five miles to the east, Vidal and his crew headed south toward Mexico twenty-five miles away. "Que manera de ganarse la vida, no?"

Vidal is not an educated man. He could not be considered an expert about American politics or economics. He doesn't concern himself with such things, but as he disappears like vapor into the mountains of the Sierra Madre Occidental he possesses a primitive yet profound understanding of the border culture. He understands that when you scrape away all of the rhetoric and political maneuvering, the real engine that powers the border culture is money. He may be a Mexican. He may not be well educated, but he plans on getting his share, and he knows that the money comes from somewhere in the middle of the United States.

Although he was threatened, Ben Moody was never indicted, charged, or arrested for a crime. He repeatedly asked for assistance from the office of Republican congressman Earnest Dolittle and from the congressman himself in acquiring a case number of the investigation in which he was the principal suspect that was questioned. He also asked assistance from the New Mexico State Police, the FBI and the U.S. Border Patrol in acquiring this information. He never received anything.

Ben asked for assistance from Congressman Dolittle, the state police, the FBI and the Hidalgo County sheriff in getting back his pistol, which was found with the one load of dope that was stopped and captured several miles north of Animas on the night that the caravan passed through the area. He was told that it was being held at a law enforcement facility in Las Cruces, but it has never been given back to him.

His cell phone was destroyed by authorities after they performed their exploration into its contents.

The story of Ben Moody's odyssey received no recognition from any major media outlet of any kind.

Made in the USA
Columbia, SC
01 May 2021